HEROIC CARE

35 Writers & Artists Show What It Means To Care

Edited with an introduction by

Betsy Ellor

Words
Unbound
Books

1

First published in paperback in US in 2021
by Words Unbound Books

Cover Design: Lauren Cepero & Betsy Ellor

Words Unbound Books
www.wordsunboundstudio.com

Contents

"The simple act of caring is heroic."

- Edward Albert

Introduction

by Betsy Ellor

S*how us what it means to care.*
This anthology started out with that simple
challenge. It was set for writers and artists around
the world. There were no genre, no length, and no form
limitations. It could be about lovers, parents, strangers,
pets, anything that might speak to readers.

I love variety. Like most readers, my love of story
extends beyond one section in the bookshop. Give me an
inspiring memoir, a good romance, a fast-paced fantasy.
I love it all. When the submissions began to roll in it was
clear that this collection would fill readers like me with
surprise and delight at both the quality and diversity of the
work.

As I assembled the final anthology, one unifying

truth emerged: To care is to be brave. The act of caring about something or someone means allowing in the possibility of not only infinite joy but also infinite pain. It is always the things we care about most which cause us the most heartache. Yet, despite that huge risk, nearly everyone chooses to care every day.

It is my hope, that in reading through these many varied interpretations of what it means to care you will be inspired to see the heroism in your own caring because all caring truly is heroic.

The Night Before Dad's Last Day

Jill Witty

His grainy, unfocused eyes track my shape in the bathroom mirror. The fog on his brain reduces me from "Joy, beloved daughter" to "unfamiliar female." I warn him of the sting to come, wash his bloodied elbow with a warm cloth, watch him grimace. He still knows pain. I wonder if it's possible to scrape a heart—if that tender organ rubs itself raw against other tissues, its forever companions— which might explain the unrelenting ache that clutches my insides. How can you heal an unreachable wound? I snug one arm around Dad's now-slender waist and shoulder him to bed.

A Block of Ice and a Small Bag of Sugar

Young Vo

I stood like a shadow in the California sun and listened as my grandmother and Mah exchanged Vietnamese words of goodbye, "Chao tạm biệt."

We stood in the driveway waving until the emptiness of someone leaving settled in.

"Your grandmother has done a lot for us. Remember? We lived with her when you were born," Mah reminded me in Vietnamese.

"I was too small to remember." My usual response. Does anyone remember where they were or what they did as a newborn?

"Let's go inside; I'll make lunch." Mah walked away without waiting for a reply. Like a shadow, I followed.

We walked through the lopsided gate and past the wall of potted plants. The air was still cool and moist from the watering that morning. Mah stopped to pull some of the dead leaves. I looked around, so many plants potted in random containers, stacked on tables and shelves. Plants in shoes, drawers, boxes, and cooking pots it was strangely comforting to see. Long red pepper and peppers that looked like berries. There was also Vietnamese basil that you put in Phở; the leaves are harder than American basil. She worked on her plants, pulled, picked, moved them around, and shook her head. Mumbling words only her plants could hear.

"Mah, I'll drive us to go eat. You don't need to cook. Just relax," I said in broken Vietnamese.

"Hmmm, that would be good." Mah walked into the house. I stood waiting in her makeshift garden.

§§§

The restaurant smelled of star anise, lemongrass, and French roasted coffee. The floor was a little sticky. Loud conversations, ceramic plates moving, chops sticks hitting and slurping, a lot of slurping. The waitress found our table and handed us our menu. I wiped down the spoons and chopsticks as Mah looked at the menu. She always ordered for us. It was less confusing for everyone.

"How are you and your girlfriend?"

"We're fine," I poured her some Jasmine tea. She tapped the table, indicating that was enough. I poured myself some tea.

"How long have you been together?" I stopped mid-pour. It was going to be a long lunch.

I let out a breath, "A couple of months…"

"What happened to your friend Becky? I liked her."

"Do you mean Betty?" I looked for the waitress. Where was the food?

"When can I meet your girlfriend?" Mah put down her teacup.

I pretended I hadn't heard.

"Does she love you?" She looked up from the table.

"I don't know. Why are you asking?" I stared at her. Hoping she would change the subject.

"Love is different when you marry," She looked off to my right and talked about a time living with her mother-in-law and great aunt. In the Spring, they went to the market to buy food and shop for the family. She said they

got a little old used dress. Mah put together a smile for her in-laws. She had to say "*Cảm ơn,*" Thank you. A good wife is grateful. A good wife does not complain.

Mah's voice shook. She paused and turned to me. I held onto my seat, thinking of what to say. I looked down at the empty spoon. She grabbed a napkin that was between us. Mah looked off to my right again. She kept on repeating that it was very hard, "*khổ lắm.*" She did all the hard work and never complained.

"Where was Bah?"

"Your Dad didn't understand," she explained. "When you marry someone, you make sure that person loves you and loves you more than their family."

The food came as she lectured about money, school, and love. I added bean sprout, cilantro, basil, and peppers to my Phở bowl. Nodding and grunting to Mah, so she knew I was listening. I wasn't. I have heard this before.

Her voice started to blend in with the other noises of the restaurant. I ate and listened to the beats of chopsticks, steps walking, chairs pushed in and out, and the cash register ringing. It was a good lunch.

As we drove from the restaurant she asked, "Do you remember Indonesia?"

"No."

"You were too small," she paused then continued, "We fled Vietnam hoping to land our boat in Malaysia. They had no room and forced us to sail to Indonesia."

"We were lucky," she said. "You and your sisters didn't get sick. Other people that came with us were sick, and some even died." She stalled in thought and then looked out the side window.

"Your father was sick. He came close to dying."

"We had to make our hut from sheets and wood from the boat. You were three. Remember? *kho'làm.* We did not have very much money. We were afraid to spend money because we did not know how long we would be there. A couple of months, but it turned into a couple of years." This time her voice cracked. She looked forward, but I could tell her thoughts were on Indonesia.

"I had to earn money. Your father couldn't work. Food was not always guaranteed at camp. Your aunt Trinh and I decided to go to the mountain to buy fruits to sell. The farther we went, the cheaper the fruits. We could leave camp during low tide; during high tide, the bridge was uncrossable. No one really left camp; we had to find our way to the farmers. The food that we could buy was tied to wooden poles and carried across our backs. We sold it in the makeshift refugee camp for a little profit."

"You know *chè đậu trắng*, the sweet rice dessert?"

"Yeah?" I said.

"Your aunt wanted to buy some. At that time, your aunt was unmarried, remember?"

She turned and smiled, but her voice was still shaky. Mah never told me this story before.

"I didn't want the sweet rice dessert." Her smile turned to tears so fast that they hit me by surprise. It stung my eyes. "I couldn't eat thinking of you and your sisters there hungry. I couldn't eat, thinking of you and your sisters, *kho' làm, kho' làm* (it was so very hard)."
Mah never bought any sweet rice dessert but instead purchased a block of ice and a small bag of sugar. She made snow cones for my sisters, my sick father, and myself.

I saw my mother with new eyes as if I was a child again, watching her feed me for the first time, seeing her bathe me for the first time. No longer the nosey woman with the questions, no longer the critical woman, but a woman from the pages of history, our history, one that holds her family together by her sacrifices.

That night I was bleeding with so many thoughts, choking on the images. I scratched into my sketchbook these words, these pictures:

Heroic Care

In the car, you looked and found Indonesia
You shook and cracked as you try to find
the words hidden in your past
On our behalf, you stepped out of safety
Walked over low tide
Made a path up a mountain
And came down with burdens tied to your back
You traded your sacrifices for a block of ice and a bag of
sugar
Like your shadow, I listened

Put your mind at ease
Your words have been heard
I will find my voice

I will remember
The long journey
Trials overcame, tears shed, wounds hidden, and the pains
buried
Let me shout in this nation of immigrants
I will utter the sounds you could not
I will speak with confidence
Unashamed of what I will say

To be your hands
To bring you pride
To fulfill your hopes
To step out of your shadow
Mah

Long-Distance Mourning

Luna Ranjit

One muggy August morning, a terse email popped up from my father, informing me that my Aji had joined the ancestors. I had just graduated from college in Iowa, and moved to Washington, DC, for an unpaid internship hoping to jumpstart a career in environmental research. Aji passed surrounded by her surviving children and all her grandchildren, except her favorite one. With no money and my international student visa about to expire, I could not even contemplate flying out to mourn with my family in Kathmandu. I quietly stepped away from my desk, sat on the bathroom floor, and bawled.

Montana Hospitality

Ian P. Owens

On a snowy Friday evening in January 1999, I stood in front of the Departures board in Detroit Metro airport, laptop case dragging down one shoulder and ruining my posture. I watched as the last yellow "Delayed" turned into red "Canceled." A blizzard of historic proportions howled outside while inside, frustrated travelers milled aimlessly. Nothing would fly this night.

In 1999 my job did not warrant a mobile phone, much less a personal assistant to jump into action whenever I called. I needed no assistant, being an expert traveler and wonderfully self-sufficient. Ruling out six hours in a cheap motel at jacked-up prices, I secured a ticket for tomorrow's early flight to Boston, then hunted down a campsite: a bench seat in a quiet corner. Hotels were for wimps. I'd save my time and money and be first in line for my flight home.

Morning sun backlit my eyelids pink after an endless awful night of broken sleep on a barely padded and sloping steel bench. No wonder they call these places "terminals," because that's how I felt: sweaty, stubbly, aching, and exhausted. Terminal. Why was I here? Not just here in Detroit Airport, but on this planet? I was not who my six-year-old self had wanted to become: either a fighter pilot or a movie star.

That question continued to gnaw at my soul as I sat wedged in "B" between two smelly Sumo-sized neighbors on the flight home. There, my fiancé, Jane wasted no time in letting me know how bad I looked, how gray I was getting, and asked how much longer did I think this would continue. I was on course to a pointless life with an early grave unless I took immediate action.

I sifted through the mail that had arrived while I was away. The new issue of "Adventure Cycling" magazine caught my eye. On the cover, a tanned and fit dude astride a bicycle loaded with gear studied a map, the endless Montana prairie spread before him, the snow-capped Rockies in the distance. He was living my dream, and I wanted to be him.

I would be him. I'd quit my job, get all that gear, and go. I'd cycle across North America, I'd ride the "Big One" and all the answers I sought would be waiting at the end of it.

"I'm coming with you," was Jane's reply to my scheme.

"I have to do this alone," I said. "This is MY dream."

Jane crossed her arms.

Three months later, springtime in Washington state, I stood astride my new bicycle, loaded with gear, studying a map. I looked back. "All set?" Jane occupied the rear seat of our new Ibis tandem. Still my dream, but our adventure.

All went well across Washington, but Idaho's panhandle had a surprise in store. A careless drink of non-potable water laid me low, my insides a seething cauldron of pain. After four days of trying to heal myself with my iron will, I'd only become more depleted, feverish, and weak with each passing day. A supreme pedaling effort got us into Montana. Somewhat delirious, I was convinced that Idaho had leveled a curse on me, and getting out of the state would fix everything. We spent the night in a ranch-style bed and breakfast, just over the state line.

"All right, all right, I'll go. I'll get us there," I said. In our room the next morning Jane and I were the nearest to an argument yet on this journey. Since my life-force missed roll call again, Jane insisted it was time to seek medical assistance. She was 105 pounds of solid obstinacy. I reluctantly agreed, but felt we needed to get there under our own power.

"Let's go talk to Alex and find out where the nearest

doctor is," Jane said. We dressed and went to see our hosts, Alex and Eileen.

"There's a clinic in Libby," said Alex, a real cowboy who could have played the part of the Marlboro man, minus the cigarettes. "That's about forty miles away. I'm not sure what their hours are."

"I'll call them," said Eileen, his cowgirl wife. "They might not be open all day on Saturdays."

A moment later she returned. "Good news. The clinic is open until noon today. Closed tomorrow, though."

"Noon?" I checked my watch: 9:25. Forty miles, cycling in my condition? "We'll never make it there by noon."

"Sure you will," Alex said. "I'll take you in the truck."

"Well, actually--" I began, but never finished.

"Thank you so much!" Jane said. No way are we going to ride in a truck! I wanted to say, This was my Big One and that would be cheating, like Rosie Ruiz riding the subway to victory in the Boston Marathon. But I had no fight left in me. Libby was along our route, and taking a truck there meant we would not technically be riding my entire Big One. Maybe we could circle back and ride those miles afterward. It made us frauds, not doing it on our own.

"We'll get packed up right away," Jane said, and off she went.

A couple hours later we waited for test results at the clinic where Alex dropped us off and wished us luck.

I sat thinking about cowboys and why aren't they called "bullmen," since "cow" is feminine and most cowboys are male and grown-up? And why don't we have a word for a male ballet dancer, like "ballerina" for the females? Would "ballerino" be the correct term? Or maybe "baller?"

A lady doctor emerged from the lab and sat across from us. She wore horn-rimmed glasses, a stethoscope, a white lab coat, and a reassuring smile. Good news, I hoped.

"It looks like you picked up a protozoan, possibly giardia." she began in that low soft silky tone meant to put us at ease. "It's easily dealt with; you're going to feel better real soon. I have a prescription for you, and you'll need to keep away from certain foods while you're on it: fats, meats, dairy, and sweets are all off-limits, I'm afraid. I made a list so you can remember."

"In other words, everything that tastes good," I said and she flashed her smile again. Fortunately, I had no appetite, and could probably live several more weeks on the midriff fat remaining from all those business trips.

We found a pharmacy in Rosauer's Supermarket in Libby and got my prescription filled, then sat down on the curb in front. Now what? Early afternoon, we should be riding to the next town, making up for lost time, but I could not. I'd never been to Libby, Montana before, and knew no one. For the first time on this journey, I just wanted Home. Jane sat beside me, silent.

I was at a loss what to do, and fought a rising panic.

A shopping cart trundled past, pushed by an elderly

lady with a kind face. Jane made eye contact and then hopped up. "Hello," she began. "We're touring the country on a bicycle and just arrived here. My husband needed to go to the clinic; he's been feeling a little sick; probably a stomach bug. Do you know of any nice places to stay in town? Someplace … homey?"

'Husband' was not technically correct. Jane was thinking fast. Her grandmother would not approve of an unmarried couple sharing a room, and this lady, being her grandmother's contemporary, probably held similar views and Jane didn't want to alienate a potential ally.

Dee Youso, steel grey hair pulled sensibly back into a bun, wore age-appropriate navy slacks and a hot pink blazer. She seemed comfortable in her seniority, a respectable elder without pretense of youth. She took one look at me and said: "The only ones I know of are motels; not very nice when you're feeling sick." She paused then, looking us both over. You could almost see the wheels turn as maternal instincts engaging.

"Listen, honey, I've got a spare room upstairs nobody's using. You're more than welcome to it."

The shock of this statement froze me in place, but Jane lit up. The women chatted pleasantly and then made arrangements. Relief and gratitude washed over me at this invitation to stay at a total stranger's home.

But I also had a pang of trepidation: what was the hidden catch? What would be asked of us in return? Would we be safe? Didn't the Unabomber come from Montana? I would stay alert. You never get something for nothing, an inner voice said.

A few minutes later we rode at ten miles per hour, following Dee's enormous powder-blue Lincoln with the Montana license plate MA&POPS, as it glided into the huge carport attached to a neat little ranch house. Her husband Al, retired, welcomed us with a big smile, as if we were his visiting grandkids. He stood tall and dignified, big hands strong and roughened from a lifetime of working with them. When his warm hand enveloped mine, I didn't want to let go. "Want to see where I do my wood work?" he asked.

Somewhere during the workshop tour, Al's gentle manner and warm enthusiasm penetrated my armor of suspicion. I forgot about being on alert and my shoulders retreated from up around my ears. Al and Dee had no hidden agenda. They lived by the Golden Rule. They took us into their simple and tidy home only because we were fellow humans, far from home, in need of a friend.

Al possessed exceptional woodworking skills; mostly nature scenes of local flora and fauna. I particularly admired a snarling cougar cribbage board carved from a single piece of Douglas Fir. Part Two of the tour took place in the Lincoln as Al drove us around town, pointing out the sites where his larger works were on display. Intricately carved bears reared up; eagles took flight, totem poles thrust skyward, and a colorful mural covering an entire wall inside of a church. It depicted their town with the image of Jesus, ever watchful, rising over the distant Rocky Mountains.

"I painted this a few years back after a medical episode. I almost died from internal bleeding. I saw all my ancestors gathered around the hospital bed, and in that moment, I knew there was a world beyond this one; a life everlasting."

"That's amazing," Jane said. "My stepfather had the same experience just before he passed. He saw people around him that we couldn't see."

"I don't fear death anymore," Al said. "I know that Jesus watches over all of us."

Al knew death, not as an ending, but as a natural transformation from matter to spirit; from seen to unseen. First-hand knowledge had confirmed his Christian beliefs. Al spent his elder years adding beauty to this world, which countless others would enjoy long after he'd passed into the next one.

We got home as Dee put the finishing touches on a simple steak-and-potatoes dinner. We regaled them with our stories from the road, as travelers have done for millennia to repay their hosts' kindness.

After dinner, Al stepped outside to light his pipe. He would not smoke it indoors during our visit.

We tucked ourselves into the twin beds in the spare room that night. "Are you amazed?" I asked Jane.

"It feels like we're at my grandma's house," she said. "It has the same smell, like family and memories; and the same peacefulness. I feel very safe here."

"That they would take us in at face value amazes me," I said. "We could be anybody."

"But we're not, and they knew it. They live in rural Montana, not Boston."

"And come from a less crazy time. A more innocent time? But the Depression and the War, was that less crazy or more innocent? Maybe it was because we knew who the bad ones were."

Silence followed. Like a little child worn out from a busy day; warm, safe, and protected at Ma 'n Pop's, I fell fast asleep.

Despite my paltry dinner, the next morning I felt like Clark Kent bursting out of the phone booth as Superman, full of energy, due to the combination of antibiotics and surrogate-grandparenting. Al presented us with a parting gift: the cougar cribbage board, which he offered to ship home to us, knowing it was way too heavy to carry. And after persistent efforts by us, they finally, laughingly told us what we could give in return: a pair of Maine lobsters. I wondered if it was possible to ship them and vowed to get lobsters to them, somehow.

We pedaled away, waving big and riding steady, while I thought about these two strangers who had become friends in less than a day. I thought about the grandparents I'd never known but wished I had. I thought about Alex and Eileen, the doctor and staff at the clinic, and especially Jane, who had pulled me out of my self-imposed and self-destructive isolation. She did that for love, of course, but what incentive did the others have? Would I have invited strangers into my home? Would I have cared whether a tourist made it to the clinic or not? What would have happened had I been alone on this journey, determined to do it all myself?

This would not be the last time we'd need help in getting across North America, but it was the last time I resisted it. Hell, I welcomed it. And we made it home.

Months later, I got those lobsters to Al and Dee.

Apricots in Afghanistan

Colleen Michaels

There ought to be an aircraft emergency card, laminated
instructions for small talkers in cases of ignorance.
I looked for one in the pocket of my aisle seat
when I sat in the last row of a flight next to a fatigued boy.
And I knew I was asking too much of him,
asking him to hold my precious skinny latte.
Still, I asked this soldier to hold as I began to spill.
So what do you do? I mean, over there? He told me it was
cold, very cold, not the dry heat you'd expect. Just cold,
like here.

I took back my paper cup, almost thanking him for his
service.
There's a good steak house in the terminal!

41

Apricots in Afghanistan

I hear the apricots in Afghanistan are great!
I told him I thought it must be funny to be seated
next to a civilian like me, unable to navigate even a cup of
coffee.
He said politely *No Ma'am, it's not that funny at all.*

The attendant leaned over me and offered him whatever he
wanted:
The big box of M&M's, Pringles, full can of Coke. *Take
them,* she said.
It's what we do for service members. You won't have to pay.
She dumped it all on my tray as the seat-belt light came on.
I was overflowing with small concessions.

Keepsake

Karen Zey

I lift the glass ball with its silver-green-red harlequin pattern from the well-worn cardboard box, the only one left from the dozen bought at Miracle Mart a lifetime ago. The baby—now a young man—doesn't remember his dad except from photos. Wife to widow to wife. I stumbled through grief and loneliness before finding love again. Before reclaiming the joy of three stockings to hang, a reflexive humming of carols, cornball family traditions. Gingerly, I hang that old-fashioned orb of sparkle on a pine branch. Glass ornaments can shatter so easily. I don't want to run out of miracles.

Snowbound

Matthew Phillion

I was smoking a cigarette on the fire escape when I heard Sherrie unlock the four locks on our front door and drag her luggage back inside.

We lived in what we affectionately called a one and a half bedroom apartment on the Lower East Side, where I inhabited a converted walk-in closet. The apartment was a fifth-floor walk-up, which meant Sherrie's ninety-eight-pound self had to carry two suitcases the whole way up.

At that moment, she was also supposed to be at the airport.

"Should I assume it's a bad sign you're here?" I asked. Sherrie bolted upright, eyes as large as an anime character's, and picked up the nearest piece of debris – an old magazine, in this case – and hummed it at the window.

"The fuck are you doing out there?" she said.
"Shouldn't you be gone?"

"You've been outside. Have you seen the snow?"

"As a matter of fact, I have, dumbass. That's
why I'm here. My flight's canceled, and there is now no
chance in hell I'll get to Los Angeles for Christmas." She
unwound a long red scarf and chucked it over the armrest
of our careworn couch, pulled her wet, snow-covered wool
hat off, and threw that in my general direction as well.
"Christmas in New York sucks."

"I know." Christmas alone in New York is even
worse, I didn't add. I started the dicey descent back into
the apartment, involving a move I saw on "The Dukes
of Hazard" as a kid. I ended up on the floor with a thud,
looking up at the ceiling. "Whyn't you call me to come
down and help you carry your shit up?"

"Have you been drinking?"

"Aye-firmative."

"So I take it you're not driving home then? I didn't
call because you're supposed to be on the Mass Pike right
now."

Sherrie stood over me, one booted foot on each side
of my head, and stared down. Her blonde hair, cut short and
parted in a hard slash to the left, was wet and brass-colored.
She offered me a hand to get up, and I took it but wasn't
really capable of helping myself much, so after a pair of
half-assed tugs, she left me on the floor and walked away.

"What the Christ have you been drinking?" she

asked. I couldn't see her, but I heard her rummaging around the half-kitchen, blocked from my view by the futon.

"Scotch."

"The Scotch I gave you for Christmas?"

"Yep."

"I gave it to you early because we're supposed to be three thousand miles apart on Christmas morning," she said.

I threw up both arms in a sort of feeble V of victory. She shook her head at me.

Sherrie walked past me again, disappearing into her bedroom. She came back out in a black hoodie and yoga pants. She put her hands on her hips, as if incapable of believing I hadn't moved from the floor.

"So you're not going home."

"Remember last time I drove to Boston in the snow? Me and my shitbox car spent the weekend in Hartford instead. Ever been stuck in Hartford?"

"No."

"Hartford is a pit."

"So I've been told," she said. "Where's the bottle? Tell me you didn't finish it."

"Of course I didn't finish it. I'm not a barbarian."

I pointed to my "room," such as it were. Sherrie wandered off again, walked back in with her lips on the bottle.

"So I've decided I could have planned my flight home better."

"Like, perhaps, not leaving on Christmas Eve itself?"

"Something like that, yeah." Sherrie sat down next to me, cross-legged, clunking the bottle between us. I looked up at her and gave her my most charming drunken smirk. She put one hand over my eyes and pushed my head in the other direction. She'd been doing that for near eight years now. When we were in college together, our roommates were dating, so, by default, we ended up in the same social circle. While our friends had already married and divorced; Sherrie and I had remained the strangely platonic perpetual roommates people made Sam and Diane jokes about.

"I think I'm going to move back to LA," she said.

"You say that every time it snows."

"Well, I fucking mean it every time it snows."

"Funny how people always say how great having four seasons are when three of them are actually pretty miserable," I said.

Sherrie reached over absently and grabbed a hold of my hair. Not ungently, she used the grip to move my head around, back and forth.

"Does alcohol actually paralyze you?" she asked.

"No," I said. "Wine gives me tunnel vision, if we're keeping score."

"No, I mean this pliability thing. You turn into silly putty when you're drunk. I could probably tie you into a pretzel."

"Please don't try to tie me into a pretzel."

"I'm not. I'm just saying. I think I could," Sherrie said.

We sat in silence for a moment, watching the snow fall outside in great white chunks. No planes would be taking off for Christmas. At this point I'd put money on Santa saying fuck it, I'll get them next year.

"Think Santa's calling the Easter Bunny right now, trying to swap delivery routes?" I joked. It was a weak joke, but at least I knew it.

Sherrie just stared at me the way one stares at a socially inept cousin, put her hand over my eyes again, and shoved me away.

"Seriously. Why didn't you leave?" she asked. "You totally could have beat the storm."

"I know."

"So?"

"I was drinking like the Irish."

"But you were drinking Scotch," she said. "I know that one."

"I feel like Big Bird in Sesame Street Christmas," I said. "Like I'm supposed to be sitting outside looking for Santa to ask him how such a big old dude gets down those skinny little chimneys."

"Who am I then?"

"I dunno," I said. "Eaten any phones lately because they look like cuppie-cakes?"

"Did you just call me Cookie Monster?" she asked.

"I may have implied."

"You suck."

"I just called myself a six-year-old, giant yellow bird," I said.

Sherrie smiled and took another pull on the bottle.

"I miss my dad," she said softly.

"I know," I said.

"I wanted to be there on Christmas morning."

Sherrie stood up quickly, went to the wall, and plugged in the pitiful set of multi-colored Christmas lights we had strung across the windows. She wandered to the front door, shut off the lights, and plopped down beside me again.

"God, if I knew we were going to be here on Christmas morning I would have bought a stupid tree," she said. "I specifically didn't buy a tree because we weren't going to be here."

I pointed at the coat rack by my room. Sherrie stared at me. I pointed again.

"Did you string Christmas lights on the coat rack?"

"Yeah, they were like thirty-five cents at Rite Aid."

"You bought lights to hang on the coat rack?"

"The hell else was I going to do? I couldn't find anyone to sell me a tree."

Sherrie gave me a hard stare, then squinted at me. It was vaguely intimidating.

"Why didn't you go home?" she said suspiciously.

I shrugged. I was starting to sober up enough to

know I probably looked like an ass on the floor, one foot resting on the radiator.

"Had a feeling they'd close the airport," I said. "I didn't want you to be alone on Christmas."

She stared at me again, this time with tiny creases forming on her brow as she squinted.

"If they didn't close the airport you would have been alone on Christmas."

I shrugged and gestured grandly at the coat rack.

"I got a Christmas tree. Coat rack. Thing. I would have been fine."

Sherrie crawled over so we were face to face, but inverted to each other. I flinched as she leaned in, expecting some sort of physical violence, or at least a hand over the eyes again. Instead, she kissed me, upside-down, lightly on the lips.

"You're a jackass."

"I've been called a lot worse."

"I've called you a lot worse," Sherrie said, nodding and smiling.

She laid down on the floor with me, her head on my shoulder, our heads ear to ear. She stretched out one leg and rested her foot on the radiator next to mine. Somewhere down the hall, someone was playing a Christmas record. Some anonymous pop star was singing "Blue Christmas."

"That's not bad for a Christmas song," she whispered. And Sherrie and I spent the rest of the night on the floor, listening to someone else's carols, waiting in the dim glow of cheap bulbs for the sound of reindeer in the sky.

Dress Blues

Kelley H. Dinkelmeyer

I bend over, picking up socks, books, a school pencil. I'll do laundry, check email, maybe start on dinner. The next thing and the next thing and the next thing to get through the day. Looking straight ahead and not too far back or too far forward – my strategy for dealing with the new normal. I straighten up, and the gut punch comes swiftly and unexpectedly. Hanging there, the blue dress she picked out herself, the one she didn't get to wear to the sixth-grade dance, stolen by a virus. I wait until I'm in the shower to cry.

Quarantine Hacks

Mandy Zhang

Social Distancing...

Who do you want to see most
when we re-open?

Wild Horses

Tammy Donroe Inman

I drag my teenage sons into the woods for a walk. The morning air is cold and silent. "I feel like galloping," I say out loud. They roll their eyes, muttering about what a stupid, embarrassing idea that is, so I just take off, fast. The younger one critiques my galloping style ("you have to clap your feet together or it doesn't sound right"). He flies past to demonstrate. The older one follows, impersonating my ridiculous, loping gait. On and on we gallop down the trail, wind in our lungs—a giggling, shrieking stampede. Has there ever been such joy?

The Canyon Riders' Code

Susanna Baird

Grover, Massachusetts, 1926

Paces upon paces behind his father, Ev was. His feet were smarting from insults enacted by stones scattered across the dirt road. Up ahead, tucked into a dip in the fields, he could see a low, white house. This must be where the old man lived, but Ev's father walked past the stone path leading to the door, instead breaking into the long grasses beyond. Once Ev reached the point where his father hung left he could see a way forward, not a proper path but grasses trampled down. The stalks on either side, August long, reached out toward Ev as he cut in, nipping at his shins.

Ev's father never turned back toward Ev to make sure he was there, kept his eyes fixed on what Ev didn't know. The old man was down below, Ev could make him out now, sitting next to a pond, small and round and cupped on one side by a curving string of low chairs. Ev watched his father's head bob, bob and bobbing, until suddenly he ducked down and turned fast toward Ev, holding out a snake.

"Hey, look here." Ev's father's voice was an invitation and sounded new to Ev, who came closer to see. The snake was an odd and attractive thing, slender and brown with yellow stripes running the full length of its body, but also it looked slippery and possibly mean, and Ev wondered at his father's nerve picking it up. He wasn't sure what to say, his father clearly waiting for something, sticking the snake towards Ev, and Ev not sure in offering or challenge. He noticed his father held the snake loosely, his hands moving a bit to keep the snake with him. Ev wondered if it was scared. Finally, his father spoke again. "You want to put both your hands around the middle of the guy, they don't like you too close to the head."

Challenge. His father wanted him to hold the snake. His mother came into his head, her admonitions against touching wild things. He guessed his father might be disappointed if he refused, but also he didn't want to feel the snake's skin, or its slither. "Come on, Ev, it's only a little ribbon snake." And when Ev still didn't reach out, he said, "You've spent too much time with the girls."

§§§

62

Ev longed to be with the girls that minute, hadn't wanted to leave them. They were back down the road, in the drafty flat-fronted house they were letting for the summer so Ev's father, who'd had a stroke that spring, could recuperate. After dinners, Ev and his mothers and sisters settled on the uncomfortable furniture in the house's front room.

First night there Ev claimed an armchair, stiff and creaking, and dragged up a spider-webby crate he found in the basement to serve as footrest, guessing correctly his mother would not mind that which would have horrified her at home. He'd found a book called *The Canyon Riders' Code* on the parlor's bookshelf, about two cowboys who skittered around the Wild West. They acted outside the law but always treated everybody with "the truest kind of respect that takes no accounting of a man's position," as the taller cowboy, Dale, liked to say, and often. Five pages in and Ev was hooked.

After they'd all settled, Ev and his mother and sisters, Ev's father walked in and Ev thought he might have to offer up his stiff seat and sit on the rag rug. But his father announced, "I'm heading down to Ernie's, back in a bit."

Soon as the door shut behind him, Ev's littlest sister asked no one in particular, "Who's Ernie?"

"The elderly gentleman who lives down at the end of the road," Ev's mother answered. Ev didn't think gentlemen lived on pressed-dirt roads, but knew not to say so. "He's an acquaintance of your father's from growing up," and she kept talking, but Ev was too engrossed in the Wild West to keep listening. So it went for several nights. About a third left of the book, Ev had settled down for another evening on the chair when his father walked in with his usual "Heading down to Ernie's."

This night, Ev's mother replied, "Take Ev with you, Jim."

Ev did not jump up, felt betrayed by his mother, but also knew his father would refuse. And he did. "The old man's a little rough, probably best Ev stays here with you ladies."

"Ev is not a child, James, he's 12 years old," and with his mother's switch to his father's full name, Ev knew he was going. "It'll be good for him to spend some time with you." She looked to Ev, nodding him up out of his seat. "Mr. Stone's a writer, Ev. Wrote that book you've been buried in all week." Ernest Stone, that was the name on the book, and now Ev was interested to see the man, but still didn't want to go with his father.

"Hop to, Everett." His father stood in the doorway, tapping an impatient hand against his thigh. Directly addressed, Ev finally scrambled up. He wasn't properly dressed for a visit, wearing only knickers and shirtsleeves, no stockings, no shoes, but his father was clearly not prepared to wait and so Ev hurried out. Once the door was shut behind them, Ev's father said, "Look, Stone's something of a wild type. Whatever he talks about, we don't need your mother or the girls hearing it." And he took of down the road, not looking back to see if Ev would follow.

§§§

Ev sucked in air and took the snake, grabbed the skinny thing around the middle and neck, and just as quick as he'd moved, the snake nipped him, tiny sharps sticking at the webbing of skin that stretched between his left thumb and forefinger. Tears came, so Ev couldn't see the snake zipping away from the spot he dropped him.

"Damn it, Ev, I told you not to touch him near the head. Jesus Christ, he's let go with the musk too, you're going to stink all night. You're going to have to get yourself cleaned off in the pond." Ev's father moved away from Ev, who knew he'd failed, who wanted so much to turn and go back to the house and squeeze himself into the uncomfortable chair. He knew he couldn't and he marched forward, long grass itching at his legs, snake's bite stinging, its musk mixing with the warm air and a muddy green smell coming off the pond.

Up close, the old man did not look like a writer but simply like the other old men Ev knew but less finely dressed, in wrinkled, cotton clothes and with white hair uncombed. A bottle of bourbon sat in the flattened grass at his feet. He stood unsteady when Ev got close, offered no words but held out a trembling hand to shake.

Before Ev moved close enough to grasp it, his father jumped in. "Christ, Ev, you can't shake his hand smelling like that. Get yourself cleaned up." The old man sat back down as Ev's father waved at the pond.

Ev knew things moved in ponds, maybe snakes, for sure frogs and fish, and grabbing plants. The thought of any of these touching him raised goosebumps along his arms and legs. He took off his knickers and his shirt, leaving his union suit on, and stepped onto a board reaching out over the water. His arms hugged his sides while his feet deliberated, rolling across the grooves in the wooden plank. His eyes considered the muck-brown of the water. He dreaded the moment when the pond stole his breath.

"For god's sake, Ev … " his father started in, but the old man interrupted.

"Oh, it's something, Ev" he said. "You won't believe the feel of it. Like sliding into something lovely." Ev stood another minute, trying to believe the old man, his father's impatience a pushing hand at his back. Finally, he jumped.

And the old man was right, it was a sliding, not the shock he expected, the pond warmer at the top and growing cooler as he slid down. He didn't open his eyes, didn't want to, felt full of the strange silence of being beneath. When something tickled his leg he shot back up, but as soon as he surfaced he missed the feeling of being surrounded by wet. He climbed out and back up onto the board. He jumped and he slid and he surfaced and he climbed and he jumped again, and even as he achieved a rhythm he occasionally broke it, standing extra minutes on the board to catch snippets of the conversation behind him.

"Spent the whole goddamned day cleaning. She's coming Thursday, thinks I can't take care of myself. You'd think she was my daughter and not my last wife."

Ev didn't know anyone with a last wife. Jump, slide, surface, climb.

"She drives me near insane, tucking all my books and such in corners so's I'm betwattled for days after."

Ev wondered if the old man's last wife was anything like Jane Endicott, the beautiful rancher's daughter in *The Canyon Riders' Code*. Although the old man must be past 70, so the last wife probably looked more like Ev's grandmother. Still, the pull of his telling was stronger on Ev than the feel of the slide, and he decided to pause in the jumping, to fill one of the empty low chairs so he could better listen.

"But Jesus, Jim, you should see the cat-heads on her. My sister told me, don't be marrying a girl so young, and turns out she wasn't wrong, but every couple months I get her shaking the sheets with me again, and …"

Ev didn't know what cat-heads were, and wasn't positive on shaking the sheets, though understood enough. Unbidden, Wallis Ann Pierce, friend of his next-up sister, appeared in his mind. A few months ago they'd all been riding, and he and Wallis Ann back to the stable before the rest. She'd kissed him, a real kiss, and pulled him hard to her. His body responded quick so he'd had to turn away. He could feel himself responding similarly now, listening to the old man to cool, he ran back onto the board and jumped. Slide, surface, climb.

From here the old man wandered, talking about a few hard cases from his early days as a dentist, a profession Ev could hardly believe given the cowboy adventures in his books; about an old cat he'd had who could, he swore, tell the future; about the time a madwoman in town, Muddy Miser, maybe Ev's father remembered her, she was still around when he was a boy, about the time Muddy Miser walked behind him all the way home, yelling he'd stolen her baby; about his editor who, the old man said, was good with the words but otherwise so dull the old man had to show up to his offices drunk to have any fun at all.

Jump, slide, and Ev found himself standing long and longer on the plank to listen to the old man's conversation, pockmarked with words Ev wasn't allowed to say, salty and verboten. A second time he headed for the chair, but this time his father noticed and shook his head no, waved him back to the board. And so he jumped, with each leap clutching a handful of words; thinking material for the seconds spent rising toward a rediscovery of air. Surface, and he'd worried he'd lost the old man's story for an unexpected bend.

Eventually, the bottle must have lightened, the night grown too dark or mosquitoes too thick, because after a slide and surface Ev climbed onto the shore to find the old man up and turned toward the house, Ev's father following behind. Ev didn't want to interrupt the rhythm he'd achieved, but knew the song ended with the old man's departure. He looked back at the pond, considering one more jump. Without the light, without the men talking, the pond once again seemed a strange and unfriendly thing. He grabbed his clothes and hurried toward the old man's house. The long grasses took advantage of his bare legs, which itched so he could hardly stand it.

By the time he arrived at the front door, the men were on the other side. He knocked, but no answer. Probably his father expected he'd return to the drafty house and his mother, but Ev wanted more of the old man's words. As he grabbed the door handle, the snake bite yelped. He'd forgotten it completely, out in the pond. The door required a shoulder shove and so hard he pushed, he stumbled into a big room that included dining and sitting and kitchen. Over everything hung a smell Ev couldn't identify, not bad but worn, like boxes brought down from the attic or the family Bible they only opened on Christmas. Across from the door, Ev's dad was sitting on the couch and the old man, back to them, was busy by a collection of bottles. Both turned toward him as he crashed, and his father spoke.

"You're getting water all over the floor, Ev. Go on home and get dry."

The old man looked at Ev, nodding him toward a pile of ratty towels stacked on the kitchen counter, near where Ev was standing. "I keep them there so they're ready when I come in from the pond. Wrap yourself up in a few,

I'll get you a drink." He did not speak with strong emotion or push, as if he was going against Ev's father, simply said the words as if Ev's father hadn't spoken at all, then turned back to the bottles.

Was he going to pour Ev a scotch or a brandy, or maybe mix him a cocktail? Several times Ev had stolen sips from bottles of brown, dreading their sting but welcoming their warm. He wrapped himself up and sat next to his father on the couch, which was wool and scratched at Ev so he had to readjust the towels. The old man delivered Ev a drink in a Mason jar, and it was ginger ale. He loved the feel of the raised glass letters and he cringed at the spice on his tongue, putting it down after only a few sips. Scratching at his hand, for the bite was still yipping, he looked around the room. So many books and he knew now this is what he smelled when he walked in, so many words on pages bound in books stretching low to high, left to right around the room. He tried to read spines, all the while his right hand bothering the bite on his left.

"Mosquitoes got you." The old man said it, not a question.

"City boy I got here, Ernie," and Ev's dad spoke as if delivering a joke. "Twelve and he doesn't know how to handle a snake, got himself chomped."

The old man didn't laugh, but moved easy his eyes from Ev's father to Ev. "Doesn't sound like a snake bite to me, Ev. What you got there is a story." With only a few words, he'd shifted the event, and now Ev's father had nowhere to go. Ev marveled. "You can see I have a book problem. Can't help myself, grab them everywhere I find them. Every book I write, I spend half of what I earn on more, by writers far better than I." Ev couldn't imagine anyone writing a book better than *The Canyon Riders' Code*, and was now even more interested in knowing what was inside these books. "Get yourself one, you can take it down the road when you go and bring it back when you're done."

Ev stood, forgetting he was only in his union suit and immediately embarrassed. Already standing and so he grabbed the closest book, not looking at the spine, and sat back down. "You a big reader?" The old man asked.

"He's always buried in a book," Ev's father said. He wasn't going to let Ev speak, clearly, but his words weren't the same poking pins they'd been up until now.

"Books are the best way to get through it, Ev," the old man said. Ev wasn't sure what "it" was. "Saved my life. Best way. Only way." He smiled thick, maybe drunk, and Ev didn't know what he was talking about but could tell the old man was feeling warm towards him. After a moment smiling back, awkward, Ev put his face down to the book and tried to read. *Pointed Roofs*, it was called, and it was about an English girl named Miriam gone to Germany to teach. The style read odd to Ev, he could tell he might like the story but he was too tired, maybe too young, to follow the words which rushed in the same pattern as they did through one's own mind. Eventually, he stopped reading

71

and closed his eyes, let his ears attach themselves once again to what the old man was saying. His sentences had grown sloppier than they were by the pond, and also they were heavier, carrying more emotion if slightly less sense.

Ev's father had kept up with the old man drink for drink, Ev had been watching, knowing his father wasn't supposed to be having liquor since the stroke. He thought about saying something, maybe referencing his mother, but to speak would be to disrupt the dance between the two men, the stories moving between the two and wrapping around Ev who, he was sure, they'd forgotten. Despite the drink, his father's words remained sharper than the old man's, though he was talking more now, too, the two of them deep into the Great War. Ev knew his father hadn't served, had been considered old for soldiering even then. The old man was telling Ev's father about this person and that they knew from long ago, people who'd gone and fought and died, and at more than one name Ev could tell his father hurt from it, maybe the first time Ev knew for sure his father felt pain from the inside. Could feel him flinch, because now Ev was nearing sleep and had propped himself up against his father. His father didn't move, didn't object.

After the third name the old man said, Ev's father tensed again, then put his arm around Ev, something Ev couldn't remember happening ever before. So tired was Ev from the swimming, so full from the stories and the books and the snake bite and the pond, so full of everything he'd lived this evening, he didn't wonder at the unfamiliar pull of his father, just gave himself up.

Cycle of Life

Elizabeth Montaño

I needed …
You were there
Feeding
Changing
Bathing
Loving
Prodding
Until …
Time to let me go
Two mothers
Friends,
A sisterhood
Commiserating
Complaining
You, lonely
Me, never alone
Feeding
Changing
Bathing
Loving
Prodding

Cycle of Life

Until …
Time to let them go
Two mothers
Children grown
Me, gray
You, silver
You needed …
I was there
The daughter
Now the mother
Feeding
Changing
Bathing
Loving
Prodding
Until …
Time to let you go
Me, alone
No changing
Feeding
Bathing
Loving
Prodding
Until …
Time for me to go

ER

Sandra Hudson

"Sandy, do you have a nine-year-old daughter?"
Hyper-alert, pulled from work's reverie, I hesitantly said,
"Yes." The voice was familiar, a co-worker, the manager
of our hospital's emergency room department. Her somber
timbre was as concerning as her words. "Could you please
come to the ER and have someone drive you?" Off-site at
the corporate office, I was cocooned from the usual hustle
and bustle of the hospital. An office co-worker drove the five
minutes to the hospital while I drowned in a kaleidoscope
of eventualities. Running through the automated doors, I
thought I was prepared, but I was not.

Two Peas in a Pod

Christi Byerly

K athryn and I would cuddle up on a big, yellow bean bag. We knew just the right way to curve our little girls' bodies, which arm over, which leg under, so we could both be cozy and comfortable.

We would start with a solid square of chocolate and each take a bite, passing it back and forth. As the square got smaller, I'd say, "You take the last bite." Kathryn would take a tiny bite and pass it back to me, saying, "No, YOU take the last bite!" I'd take an even tinier bite and pass it back, "No, YOU take the last bite." Our bites would get so, so tiny that we couldn't even see any solid specks of chocolate left. We'd end up laughing and licking each others' fingers.

In high school, we both loved to act. My senior

year, Mr. VanTol called Kathryn and me in to gravely give us the news. Kathryn had gotten the part I wanted and I hadn't gotten any part at all. I felt elated and gave Kathryn a huge hug! My little sister was going to have so much fun acting in the play! The role was perfect for her! Kathryn immediately burst into tears. As our acting teacher stood there scratching his head, she begged him, "Please let Christi be in charge of props, or be your assistant director, or something. It's her senior year, and I would feel awful if I went to play practice night after night, leaving her at home."

After college, Kathryn and I got married in a double wedding. Kathryn's husband, ever proper, said, "I don't want any cake smashing," so the two of us smashed cake in each other's faces instead. We both doubled over laughing. Kathryn rolled her eyes at me, "Husbands!" I still have a glowy photo of that moment, her eyes brilliant as she licks the cake off my fingers.

After Kathryn's divorce, I rented my sister a beautiful retreat home in Wales where she could journal, cry, and take long, healing walks on the beach.

Then, I got a phone call from an unknown number in Wales.

"Can you talk to your sister? She's ruined the carpet. All of the hand-blown glass is broken. Kathryn sent the cat dish flying through a window, and now she can't stop screaming. She's bleeding a lot. We've called an ambulance, but she's refusing to allow herself to be taken to the hospital."

"Hey, Kathryn. How are you doing?"

"I'm so amazing! I know I sound crazy, but everything I'm saying is true! It's more true than anything I've ever said. Christi, you have to help me. This is going to be the most amazing experience. The goddess of the universe told me that the whole world must sing together at the same time. You and I must call the whole world and we'll all sing in harmony at midnight. I need you to trust me. I can handle the music part, but I need your help calling everyone together. You'll handle all the time zones, and getting the different leaders on board. But it's got to be tonight!"

My heart went still. As I turned to stone, I managed, "Kathryn, that sounds wonderful. In fact, the Pope called for something similar just yesterday - a call for the whole world to pray. Kathryn, how much sleep have you gotten?"

"Why are you asking about sleep!? Christi, this is important! I haven't slept for four nights because I've been getting this amazing download straight from the goddess. I know we have to do this. We have to do this now! Please trust me. Please trust me! They're trying to drug me. They're trying to put me in an ambulance, and the goddess told me NO! NO to the hospital. That will ruin everything. They are just going to drug me. Please, Christi, please! You're the only one who really knows me. You're the only one who will believe me. Please, I know I sound crazy, but this is the sanest I've ever felt in my life. It's all real."

81

"Kathryn, it's beautiful. I will help you. I'll keep talking with you as you get in the white car. Don't worry about the hospital. They just want to make sure you can sleep tonight after we sing. You sing me the song as we go. I trust you, and you trust me, so you can go with the doctors. They just want you to get some sleep after we sing at midnight."

Driveway Birthdays

Marla Yablon

When Avi was born in the
Spring, the garage door
Was pristine, but

Two bubbles had already
Formed. We sat in
Groups on the driveway

Together, yet separate; stretching
The bonds of family,
Yearning across the pavement.

The birthday banner in the
Fall was Sarah's as
Two sparkled to three, and

Princesses and cupcakes reflected
The colors draped across the
Garage above piles of presents.

And our bubbles split to
Three as we passed
Through October, leaves blowing

Around the Legos as Rhys
Turned twelve and Mikaela's
Sweet sixteen drove by on Halloween.

The banner faded and drooped,
Wind tattered, through the
End of the year until

Straightened for the oldest,
As Grandma turned seventy,
Neither as bright as they began.

Leaving Me

Jill Pabich

Staring into the cabinet. Not seeing the beans, tomato cans, or expired sauces. Instead, I see her long wheaten hair, now blackened and frayed by too many boxes of dye. I once called it spun gold. She shouted "Nose bungled!" angrily. The word shuffle tickled me, and by repeating it I earned her annoyance. Freckles from the sun, big blue eyes like a Kewpie doll's. I see her laughing and drawing, always drawing, at the bar in front of the sink where I do dishes. I start to cry, hard, and the beans get wobbly. She is moving out today.

Check Up

Susan Klobuchar

You are downstairs in the early morning light, bare feet curled under you, reading today's headlines on your laptop. You love this time of day, the quiet before the normal flurry of she-took-the-last-waffle and mama-where's-my-binder and hurry-up-you're-going-to-miss-the-bus. But nothing is normal right now.

It was early February when you'd first heard about the virus. One of your company's executives — a blustery ex-football player with hands like slabs of meat — was the first to make it real during a work happy hour at a swanky local bar. He'd been visiting his daughter on the west coast, he'd said, and "that virus is all anyone out there could talk about!" He'd popped fistfuls of wasabi peas and regaled your colleagues with anecdotes about fellow travelers

87

donning masks on planes. "Never thought I'd see that in America!" he'd boomed, and everyone had laughed. Now he is gone, and no one is laughing.

You close your laptop, forcing yourself to end your incessant doom-scrolling, and pull out your journal. Every day you write down five things to be grateful for. When you look back at the pages written by your former self, your January and February self, the items feel foreign to you. A movie date with your husband, back-to-back screenings in a darkened theater with salty buttered popcorn. A child's school performance, proud parents clustered in folding chairs around the risers in the elementary gym. A girls' weekend with friends, laughter pealing through a hotel lobby bar.

But now, you use the journal to track the virus. How many illnesses. How many deaths. What's open, what's closed. What the government is saying, doing, failing to do. Your pencil scratches across the page, memorializing, marking the march of the virus toward you. You still capture your gratitude daily, pinch it out of the air, pin it down on the page. But the things you are grateful for are different. Smaller, maybe, but more meaningful. Flour and toilet paper in stock at the grocery store. A canister of Clorox wipes you found, forgotten in the back of your cupboard. The chirp of your child, on the stairs behind you.

"Bunny!" You smile, as she squeaks again and skitters across the floor toward you.

Your youngest is an early bird, like you, always the

first one of her siblings to wake. The squeaking is vestigial, a remnant from her baby days. She's six now, and while you know that you should discourage this habit, you also know that this is not a time for shoulds. The last time she saw her school, her teacher, her friends, was March 13, a day when your journal records gratitude for a governor who closed your state's schools. Now it's two months later, and you are scratching in your journal that there are close to 100,000 cases in the U.S., that the New York Times is running a list of the dead on its front page. It's harder to feel grateful. But there is always this child of yours.

"Good morning," you whisper to her, heart of your heart, a child whose honey blonde hair is starting to darken, whose too-short pajamas are festooned with flowers. She dances toward you, climbing into your lap. You nuzzle her neck, the smell of her, warmth and sleep and the slightest tinge of pear-scented shampoo from her bath the night before. "How did you sleep, darling girl?"

"Tomato checkup?" she asks, pointing outside. You nod, acknowledging your new morning ritual. These days are all about rituals, adding structure to days that inherently have none. You lift her off your lap and unlatch the sliding door that leads out to the deck.

In the first days — when what was happening in China and Italy still hadn't felt like something that could really happen here — you'd hauled your old self-watering vegetable planters out of the garage, where they'd lain dormant since last summer. You'd cleaned them off, put them out on the deck, filled them with soil and water. Your husband had rolled his eyes when you'd prattled on about shutdowns and shortages and buying tomato and pepper seedlings, just in case. But he'd done it, and you'd worked side by side to make a home for those baby vines in the fresh dirt.

That was before, you think, stepping outside onto the deck's still-dewy planks, Bunny at your side: before the stay-at-home orders, before masks, before you understood what "community spread" meant. Before the football-playing executive had died — on a ventilator, a colleague had whispered over Zoom, alone. Back then, it was barely spring, and you'd needed to wrap kitchen towels around the cherry tomato seedlings at night to keep the frost at bay. But now they've taken hold, their roots strong, and the daily checkup that you do with your daughter is one of the scant blessings of these fractured days.

Outside, Bunny is delighted, hopping from foot to foot as she inspects the forest of green that explodes from each planter. Days of rain have made the stems raucous and unwieldy, towering above her. She peers inside to see cluster upon cluster of green cherry tomatoes, some tiny, some fat, transforming from the dainty yellow flowers that first sprouted there. You'd never known that before now, that tomatoes came from flowers. Now, you monitor them so closely that you can tell when a new bloom is about to sprout, when its dying leaves will wither and reveal a small, resilient bud.

"Oooh, mama!" your daughter exclaims, pointing. You look, and sure enough, one cherry tomato is changing, its hue having transformed from green to red. Had it happened overnight? Or had it been flush with new color yesterday, and you'd missed it?

"Do you want to try it?" You reach forward, snap it off the vine, grateful. You'll capture this in your journal, you think. The splendor of one ripe cherry tomato, red and firm and perfect.

Bunny nods, claps her hands, as you offer the tomato to her. She inspects it, green eyes wide. You think of wasabi peas, the executive, his daughter. You wonder if she can ever be grateful again.

Your daughter places the cherry tomato in her mouth gingerly, smiles with her whole being.

You marvel at what you have grown.

Seasons of Moms

Celine Mai

Seasons of Moms

YOU WERE BORN ON A CLEAR SPRING DAY AND LIFE WAS NEVER THE SAME AGAIN.

UNDER THE WARM SUMMER SUN, WE LAUGHED, PLAYED AND LEARNED TOGETHER.

IN THE CHILL OF AUTUMN, YOU SET OUT TO EXPLORE THE WORLD ON YOUR OWN.

BUT WHEN WINTER CAME, YOU RETURNED TO THE PLACE CALLED HOME AND HELD MY HAND AGAIN.

Celine Mai

Brigham's

E.M. Panos

When I was young, my mother and I sat at the Brigham's counter on Saturdays for lunch. She made sure to sit on a stool that offered a full view of the mall outside the restaurant. We talked about my week at school or a movie we planned to see. Suddenly my mom would say "There's your husband!" I would spin around to see the most unattractive man walking by and squeal my protest. We laughed loudly enough that other customers would turn to stare. "I have fond memories of those times with my mom," I tell my beautiful wife.

Silence of Sound

Betsy Ellor

She was there. If not, he wouldn't be. There were much better ways to earn cash for college than running cases of beer up from the roach-infested basement and fighting through music fans to clean up puke and collect empties. He got all the gross with none of the tips or flirts the bartenders enjoyed. Mind-blowing music almost made up for the stench of stale booze and the writhing sweat of a dancing human mass, but really, he clocked in for her.

She wasn't cake-make-up flashing cleavage for tips like the other bartenders. She was an ash-blonde-blunt-cut-green-leg-warmers girl. She didn't need makeup; she had a spark.

Her shift started with the opening band who blasted

away any chance to talk. Still, the slightest flutter of muscles at the corner of her eye said so much, if he paid attention. And, oh, how he paid attention. The warm, spiced smell of her, the tickle of her breathe at his neck as she reached past him, the pulse under her skin as they bumped and jostled in their three-foot deep space behind the bar. Little by little she revealed herself. Gentle mimes to tell him what she needed grew into wordless comments on everything going on around them.

The club played it all. Pop bands on their way up and rock legends on their way down. Each band came with a different human mass. Some nights hippies swayed and twirled like living wind chimes. Other nights the audience wore head-to-toe black and stood motionless except for slightly bobbing heads. Ecstatic teens bursting at the naive seams with the thrill of their first-ever concerts. Equally ecstatic moms'-night-outers flaming fast as they tried to get a year's worth of wild into one night. Rock stars slid down banisters, crowd-surfed across the dance floor, and belted out lyrics stradling drinks on the bar. He and she discussed it all silently with twitched lips, wrinkled noses, tilted chins, or laughing eyes.

When the best songs played—the ones everyone in the club had come to hear — no one bought drinks, so she danced. She danced not for attention, but as if the vitality inside her needed release. In those moments the words formed on his lips, desperate to push their way into her ear to ask her to meet him somewhere they could be more than mute. But when he opened his mouth, watching her, he found he could not breathe. Then she laughed and poked him until he danced too and the moment was lost.

After a year he still hadn't found words. He wanted the perfect phrase in the perfect moment to say everything he felt. Instead, it happened as he was loading the night's trash into a dumpster.

That evening a new band performed the first gig of what would be a meteoric rise to fame. She and he danced inside music that made them feel like they had not truly been alive until that moment.

The sound still pulsed through him as he stood by the dumpster, the stench a thick and viscous wave around him as she stepped out of the back door two feet away. Her keys jangled from delicate fingers on the way to her car. Then she shivered, the night air chill after the living heat of the club. He imagined goosebumps dimpling her hidden flesh and his chest split open with need.

"Dinner?" he shouted.

His bellow echoed in the dark alley. His ears, still ringing from the club, burned bright red. He imagined himself diving into the dumpster and never coming out.

She smiled, "Of course."

They chose a date. He picked her up, surprised to see her wearing cut-off denim and a chartreuse tank top rather than bartending blacks. She looked different but she sounded the same as every word he had never heard her speak. Every story, every topic simply applied

101

consonants and vowels to all that he already loved about her. Completely unknown and yet inevitably always - he tingled with the magic of their new familiar. All the hours of wordless discussions showed him more about her than she could ever say.

Except whether she felt the same.

The joy of each moment hung suspended in fear of that question until dinner turned into drinks, turned into sitting in the car for an hour outside her place, turned into sweaty palm hoping, praying until she said, "Do you want to come up?"

"Of course," his words choked so quietly she laughed. They laughed.

They laughed and they kissed and he woke not believing he was still in her bed. Even more shocking she was in his bed the next day and the day after that. Each day a new-made miracle.

Kissing then cooking then movie nights in. Buying a duvet, a couch, a dog. Days flowed into years, into careers and shopping for a house, a lawnmower, a crib, a double stroller. "If you could do anything . . ." turned into "Can you pick up . . ." Partners adrift in a cacophony of to-do lists, reminders, party invites, parenting advice, news, Instagram, Twitter, celebrity gossip, must-watch lists, must-do lists, must-have lists, WebMD, report cards, shopping lists. So much to debate, discuss, decide, plan. Words and words and endless words.

Then one morning there was an ad for that band,

"You know, that one, from that night by the dumpster."

"I can't believe they're still touring."

"It's at our old club. We should go."

"Of course!"

But they almost didn't. Such a late-night. Sitters are expensive. The baby might be coming down with something and you know you have that big meeting the day after.

In the end they rallied. She dug in the back of the drawer to find a shirt she hadn't worn in years. He put a can of Red Bull in the glove compartment so he could stay awake to drive home and they went.

They got there early - parking was always a nightmare. They sipped wine at a nice sushi place, watching college kids outside their club scarf pizza standing on the sidewalk.

The opening band was good, but not good enough to stop watch-glances and phone checks to see if the sitter called. They made nervous conversation at the break each fought the desire to say 'Maybe we should just head home."

With an exit excuse perched on his lips, the lights lowered. The swell of that song blew his words away. Praying thanks for a band that had not lost their power he and she screamed cheers into crashing waves of sound that pulsated against their ribs and ears, drowning all other sensations. The beat pushed against their hips and legs, driving them to move, to dance. Eyes closed. Breathing and shifting in harmony. Connected only to each other,

present only in the palpable experience of the music.
Unified completely within the silence of sound.

Hannah in the Garden

Beth Anne Cooke-Cornell

In spring,
you uncover
the forsythia
from burlap
and inspect
your autumn
handiwork.
You rake
the mulch
from the roses
and work
the beets
and the carrots
into the soil
with your
cracked nails.
Your bent feet
tread the
garden paths,
as you
contemplate
succession
and yield.

But one day
the weeds
breach the defenses
and the forsythia
chokes on its breath.
You don't bother
to shut
the screen door then;
you only press
your skull
hard against
the cool floor
of the kitchen
and push your fingers
deep into your ears,
seeking out the pain,
committing
to the urgency.
You hear the scream
of your blood
in your eyes,
and taste
warm pennies
in your mouth.

When it's all over,
the bees return
to tend the garden;
the tomatoes
split their skin.
The air reeks
of dirt.

The Last Caretaker

Matthew Phillion

K4-R3's joints squeaked a bit as he made his way down a dark corridor of the space station he called home. The android sent an automated work order to himself to lubricate his knees and elbows. Part of his role was to be unobtrusive and not disturb the station's residents. The life support systems had failed fifteen years ago, and there were no humans to disturb anymore, but K4-R3 knew only the job he was programmed for. So he cleaned, and made beds, and waited once more for the sound of life and laughter to fill these slowly dimming hallways.

This Is the Day I Die

Ellen Symons

I woke knowing. When the committee knocked at the door they found me clean, dressed, my hands folded in my lap as I sat, waiting.

The chairperson holds out a letter. I unfold it: *Dear Citizen. The Committee is here to inform you…* I don't need to read more. I drop it on the side table; a table that soon, along with my living space, will be sterilized, made ready for another resident.

My few journals, my sketches, my unfinished knitting, will be of no use to a new owner and will be incinerated. My private thoughts, the tiny, flashing jewels of my dreams…those will end with me.

Her back straight, flanked by two assistants, the chairperson offers me time to prepare. But I have nothing

109

left undone. My completed scientific research went to the central database last week. My home is orderly. When I stand to leave, she insists first on explaining the procedure step-by-step. Citizens must be informed and consenting.

I am informed. I am consenting. I walk one steady step ahead of her down the long corridor to the Exit Wing. It is exactly as she told me it would be. Doors buzz open. We pass into a small room. She shakes my hand, almost meets my eyes, steps away. The door closes quietly behind her. Alone, I take off my clothes, step into a disinfecting shower.

I step out the other side and slide into a sterile paper suit. The doctor smiles. I lie on a metal table, feel the intravenous needle poke my skin, close my eyes.

Bright images from a distant past flash against my lids. My childhood was a beaded necklace of sleepless nights and anxious days. Droughts, floods, devastating storms, failed crops, drowned boatloads of humans desperate to escape misery; all of what used to be called *the climate emergency* and now was simply *life on earth* was my personal collection of worry beads. So, barely old enough, barely finished with my education in environmental science, I was among the first to join during the government's early recruiting drives. *Civil Servants Save Citizens.*

We joined to work in science, in communications, in support roles. For a per diem, all meals, and a small living unit, we swore to give our passion and our best mental efforts to improving life for everyone. Not just administrators, but soldiers—superheroes, they told us—in a battle for the survival of the species—of all remaining species—we pledged ourselves to the greater good.

And found ourselves groomed for success in a way much different than we had anticipated.

It was in another letter, all those years ago, that I learned I had been accepted. *Dear Citizen. The Committee is pleased to inform you...* I read carefully, read again, delight and bright hope rising as my fingertips stroked the watermarked pages. *Citizens must be informed and consenting.* I memorized the details of travel to my new off-planet home, packed a few belongings, fiercely hugged my loved ones, and left for the long trip to the newest colony.

In our 20s, 30s, and a few youthful 40s, our wave of bureaucrats brought a bubble of idealistic excitement into the assembly hall where orientation was held. We were interviewed, signed the employment contract, then came together to recite a heartfelt pledge to benefit all beings every day. My voice rang out.

Abruptly, dreams of camaraderie and joint effort ended. Separated, we were processed, disinfected, examined, and either sent left, down the long corridor (*to the Exit Wing*, I heard whispered), or right, into living quarters.

It has been a lonely life, but not terrible. We do our work, which has meaning. In corridors, around the edges of curfews and solitary meals, we smile, form feathery friendships. Separation keeps us from feeding each other's fears and discontent. At least I have been privileged to be kept at a peak of physical health, and to avoid the food riots and wasting poverty of the masses of citizens on the planet.

My body and brain are heavy now. My eyes are shut like the lids of iron chests. I want to fling them open, for one glimpse of the ceiling above, of the doctor's smile, of anything other than the dark inside of my skull. But I've waited too long. I cannot move.

I don't feel sorry for myself. Anymore. I've used my brain to solve problems for the good of all beings; and there is no question that the number of humans alive has crushed the planet. Numbers must be controlled. Longevity is not for all. Some of us must play my role. I have served. I will serve.

My organs and body parts will improve the future of many who haven't had the fortune of my DNA, of my pampered existence. What more should I want? A love of life is why I joined the civil service.

Reduce, reuse, recycle is the only way life survives.

Hang Up

Jill Pabich

The Trash Collector's Wife

Beth Price Morgan

Some of her spells fizzled like fat on a griddle. Others floated: luminous, full of whispered promises, before shattering like blown glass. The witch's apprentice swept them into the gutter, rubbed her tired knucklebones, and tried again. Years later, when she was a seasoned witch with many dazzling, sleek-coated spells in her drawers, she found them. Tied together like broken shoelaces and garlanded along the eaves of a small cottage at the edge of town. "Why?" the witch asked the woman of the house. "Because all hope is beautiful," the woman replied. "Even especially the hopes that never come true."

Soul Cycle

Lara Bujold Clouden

Nagini was tending five lights today. That number was high, but one of them was dimming. It wouldn't be long now — probably tonight. She picked up the transfer kit, trying to recall if she'd refilled it already. The barrel was cold to her fingertips and vibrated slightly. Yes, it was fully loaded.

She could hear Rafsan in his own quadrant, speaking softly to one of his charges. His work area was directly across from hers, on the other side of an intersecting web of looping, golden pathways. This open-air policy was new. It was supposed to encourage camaraderie and idea sharing, but Nagini tried not to listen. The conversations were too personal.

On the bench beside Nagini, one of the newer lights

stretched. She attended to it, murmuring, "Yes?"

"Grass," it said, "in the backyard… cool on my feet.
I left my shoes…"

"That sounds very soothing," Nagini said. "Why
don't you take a little stroll and enjoy it?"

The light flickered a few minutes, then shone
steadily.

"How was your walk?" Nagini asked.

After a pause, the light replied, "It's too cold to go
outside. I'm staying by the fire."

"Ah, the grass is gone?"

"Deep snow covers the grass. And it gets dark early.
My grandmother made me an afghan…"

"Take your time," Nagini said, pleased by its steady
bright glow. This one would have many passages to process
and would be with her a long time.

On her other side, next to her on the bench, the
dimmest light in the group pulsed weakly. Its voice was
faint as it said, "My mother sings to me."

"Can you see her?" Nagini asked.

"No," the fading light said. "I feel her, though. She
laughs when I kick my legs."

It is remembering the womb, Nagini thought. As she
had suspected, this dim light had reached the final stage.
The memories did not empty in order, but they always
ended at the beginning.

"She wants you to sleep and grow," Nagini replied
and smiled at the ebbing light. It was very faint now. She

put her hand beneath it and coaxed it onto the transfer platform that lay across her lap. "She loves you."

"Yes," said the light, its voice barely audible.

"Do you remember anything else about your life? You said you had a brother. You liked to swim with him?"

"No," said the light, reduced to an echo. "I remember nothing."

With one last pulse, the light went out. Only the fragile skeleton of a globe remained where the light had shone. Nagini aimed the nozzle of the transfer cartridge and pressed the release mechanism. A stream of blue smoke sparkled into the globe. It began to spin slowly, then faster until it lifted off the platform.

This was the critical moment. Nagini had never lost one, but her heartbeat quickened every time.

She set the transfer cartridge aside and stood, supporting the platform in both hands. Using it to repel the spinning globe, Nagini guided it towards the giant gold tangle suspended in the center of the room. Across the hall, Rasfan stood. He watched the orb rise, made the sign of the united sphere with his hands, and bowed his head in prayer.

Holding her breath, Nagini nudged the rotating globe toward one of the swaths of the tangle. It hovered for a moment, then attached to the strip and joined its spiraling path. The journey ended at the center of the tangle, where the globe slowed its rotation to a stop. With a bright flash it disappeared, leaving a puff of smoke.

Ragini made the sign of the sphere and touched her

forehead. She looked at Rafsan.

"I liked that one," she said. Her eyes were shining.

Every time they left, the grief exhausted her. But it was mixed with exhilaration—the beginning of a new life always moved her.

And I Have A Girl

Susanna Baird

The poster said missing.
The news said drowned.
The neighbors said the pull at high tide
where the creek meets the ocean
was something else altogether, a something
you had to respect, but something
you'd never shake hands with. Something
that when it showed up, you turned and walked away.
The news said she drowned and the mother
made the poster and the poster said missing.
When the poster was new I looked at the girl
straight-on. I am a mother and I have a girl.
I said I can only imagine.
I said I cannot imagine.
Summer peaked and the poster grayed.
I am a mother. I could not look
at that girl anymore. I did not say
anything. I pretended
she was no longer there.

Transplanted

Betsy Ellor

I lived in the sun. Sat close with my neighbors. My son's gang ran bold. Until…The economy dragged us deep where virginia creepers ascend trees that loom like my problems: find the least worst house, fix the roof, fix the fence, fix my son who rages and cries. I fit in like an invasive species. I cannot let us wither. Rise an inch with each hello. Grow a leaf when my son smiles fresh from school. Tighten one tendril as sounds in the new dark night no longer startle. Slowly I creep from the underbrush ascending towards the sun.

Summoning Love

Amos J. Landon

Mr. Jones heard his wife singing in bad Latin among the other kitchen noises through the door. His stockinged feet rested on the ottoman before the small fire in the living room. He laid his head back, resting his more-salt-than-pepper hair against the back of his favorite chair.

Mr. Jones and his wife had lived a contented life in their thirty-two years of marriage. They had moved from their tiny first apartment to this three-bedroom house right after their first anniversary. He had worked his way far enough up in his career that making ends meet had stopped being a struggle long ago. After several years and four miscarriages, the other two bedrooms remained empty. When the doctor said to stop trying, Mrs. Jones took the news with grace. The next day she inquired at the church about joining the choir. She found a sewing circle two streets down. However, as of late, Mrs. Jones seemed to be walking through her days in a mist of quiet sadness.

A yelp from the kitchen disrupted his ruminations, followed by unusual smells wafting through to the living room. "Is everything alright, Mrs. Jones," he asked.

He thought about getting up to check on her, but he rarely entered the kitchen, except to get a glass of milk in the night when his indigestion bothered him. Perhaps she was trying a new recipe. He heard a clanging noise and some coughing through the door. She did not answer.

After a time, he heard Mrs. Jones's voice call out someone's name. Gloria, was it? Did they perhaps have a neighbor by that name come to call? He could wait no longer. His curiosity and concern were getting the best of him.

"Mrs. Jones!" he called. "Mrs. Jones is anything amiss?"

Upon receiving no answer again, Mr. Jones rose from his chair and went to the kitchen. "Mrs. Jones," he pressed the door but it would not budge. He could just see her face through the opening, "Why will you not answer me?"

On the other side, Mrs. Jones pressed her slight body against the door, blocking his entrance. Her head was held high as usual, but her eyes brimmed with tears unshed.

"What on earth is the matter?" Mr. Jones asked.

"Something..." she stopped to swallow and looked over her shoulder as she spoke, "something terrible has happened."

Her tone made him look at her, carefully, for the first time in a very long time. "Tell me what has happened."

"I'm afraid it was entirely my fault."

"What is?"

"Latin is a dangerous language, Mr. Jones!" As her voice broke, the tears poured over her lids and down her cheeks.

Mr. Jones looked with concern at his, usually calm and sensible wife. "Please, Mrs. Jones, what has happened?"

"I accidentally summoned a demon!" Her hand flew to her mouth as if to unsay the words.

"You what?" Mr. Jones puffed up his cheeks in disbelief.

Mrs. Jones took a slow breath and looked at her husband. She wondered what he would think of her after this. Her tidy kitchen lay behind her. The tidy life she had created surrounded her. Somehow it all seemed damp with a loneliness she couldn't quite shake. Mrs. Jones seemed to be the only one who could see it.

Mrs. Jones told her husband how she had begun taking out the necessary ingredients for dinner. She laid out the linguine, the salt, oil, garlic, and various herbs beside the stove. She plunked a full pot of water on the back burner to boil and set the frying pan onto the front.

With some effort, Mrs. Jones managed to twist open a jar of anchovies. Carefully scooping several of them out with a fork, she set them onto a cutting board on the kitchen island.

She turned on the front burner and began to sing a Latin choral song. She didn't know all of the words, so she made them up as she went along.

"Glo-o-o-o-o-oria! Eeee-vo-co fae-le-e-e-es!"

She poured a circle of salt into the pan like she always did and then poured in some oil.

WHOOSH!!!

Orange-yellow flames shot up nearly six feet into the air. With her heart racing, Mrs. Jones grabbed a cover and smothered the blaze. Smoke filled the kitchen. She pushed open the door to the garden and carried the still smoking pan outside.

Back in the kitchen, the smoke had mostly cleared. There she found, to her horror, a great, black demon! She froze, unsure of how to proceed. She had never encountered a demon before, but there it was, eating her anchovies.

The creature was black as night and filthy, except for what appeared to be its white ears. Mrs. Jones was sure the ears were simply a spell of some sort to hide its horns. It had four legs, claws and fangs, and a long tail. There was an evil, evil gleam in its eyes. And the smell, oh it reeked of the deepest, filthiest pit of Hell itself.

She thought back to the Latin song. "Mrs. Jones! You know better than to make up words in Latin!" she muttered to herself.

She had to banish the demon before Mr. Jones discovered it. What is your true name, demon?" she asked.

The beast contorted its body and began to lick itself in a most unseemly way.

"You insult me, demon." She replayed the events in her mind, trying to come up with an answer. "Gloria!" she said at last. "Your name is Gloria. I was singing that song when I summoned you. Now I shall be rid of you, you offensive fiend."

Mrs. Jones squared her shoulders and put her hands in front of her, palms facing the demon. "I banish you back from whence you came, Gloria!" she declared.

Nothing happened. The demon didn't even look up from its licking.

She tried again. "Gloria, beast from Hell, be gone from this place!"

This time the creature moved, but only to lie down on the island and close its eyes.

"It's name is apparently not Gloria," Mrs. Jones said to her husband. "And then you came to the door, Mr. Jones."

"Alright, Mrs. Jones, let's see this demon," Mr. Jones said

Mrs. Jones hesitated, then eased the door open so Mr. Jones could peek around it. She slowly let him edge his way into her kitchen and he stopped just inside.

Mr. Jones looked closely at the filthy creature still

lying on the island next to the nearly empty anchovy jar.
Throughout Mrs. Jones' tale, he had wondered about her
sanity, but it truly was a vile-looking thing.

"We should try to push it out the back door?" he
said.

"No!" She looked at him, shocked. "We can't
send the demon I summoned out to run amok around the
neighborhood. What if it decides to go ahead and possess
poor Mrs. Walker? Or what if it eats one of the neighbor's
children?" she whispered loudly. "We must keep it here
until I can banish it back to Hell, and who knows how long
that could take. It may be years."

Mr. Jones felt an odd weight in his gut. He looked
closely at his wife of more than three decades, and the
weight grew heavier. She had never complained, not a
single time, about their lives being just the pair of them.
She had asked, only once, for a dog or cat to keep the mice
away. Mr. Jones recoiled now at his response to her plea all
those years past. If we have mice, set a trap, he had said. He
realized now how much it meant for her to have something
to look after. She asked for so little, and he was a fool of a
husband. All she had wanted was a pet. They could have
had a nice black lab. Now they had this sulfurous ball of
mats and tangles. He sighed deeply.

"Then you should probably close the door." He
nodded toward the door, standing open to the back garden.

She rushed over and slammed it shut. The demon
startled at the noise and let out a deep yowl. The horrid

sound made Mr. and Mrs. Jones jump into each other's arms.

When they found themselves in this unusually intimate position, in the kitchen no less, Mrs. Jones smiled awkwardly up at her husband. He cleared his throat and gently let her go. Turning back to the predicament at hand, he asked, "What should we do with it now?"

"Well, I suppose we must teach the thing some manners," she said. Mrs. Jones pointed at the demon. "That is quite enough of that, demon. If you are to live here, I will not tiptoe around you."

The demon looked at her, impassive.

"This won't do. You smell bad, demon. I will not have you stinking up my lovely furniture with the scent of Hellfire. You must have a bath." She turned to her husband. "Will you help me, Mr. Jones?"

In all their years together, he could think of only a few times she had asked him for help: a flat tire, a broken chair leg, a leaky sink. His heart felt heavy and warm at once.

"I'll help, Mrs. Jones," he said.

With determined kindness, Mrs. Jones picked up the demon by the scruff of the neck and carried it, snarling loudly, to the guest bathroom. Mr. Jones followed. She closed the door behind them and set the demon on the floor. The demon looked around and hopped up onto the vanity to watch the goings-on.

Uncertain of his part in these proceedings, Mr.

Jones stood back as Mrs. Jones started the water in the bathtub and readied a bottle of shampoo. She laid a towel on the floor beside the tub and another, folded beside it for drying the smelly demon.

"I hope it doesn't ruin the towels, Mr. Jones," she said. "It really does smell bad."

"Perhaps, a conditioning rinse as well would help," Mr. Jones replied helpfully.

"Excellent idea, Mr. Jones." She reached for the conditioner and set it next to the bottle of shampoo.

Mr. Jones picked up the demon. It smelled foul and it looked at him with suspicious eyes.

"Ready, Mrs. Jones?" he asked.

Mrs. Jones looked at her husband. "Well, I've never bathed a demon before. I suppose I'm as ready as I can be."

Mr. Jones leaned over and set the beast into the water. In the next twenty-two minutes, Mr. and Mrs. Jones learned what Hell looked like. The screech that came forth from the demon's throat was unlike anything they had ever heard. It tried to escape the bath, but Mrs. Jones held it by the scruff. She poured water over its fur and it raked her forearms from elbow to palm with its claws.

After a few minutes, it froze stock still and just seemed to vibrate. Mrs. Jones began to lather it with shampoo. From ears to tail, it was brown with filthy foam and swirls of loosened fur. She realized she still needed to give it a conditioning rinse. She looked down at her bleeding arms and sighed, then picked up the cup and began to rinse the quivering fiend. This caused it to climb up the side of the tub and onto Mrs. Jones's shoulder.

Still covered in foam, the demon clung to her flesh with his claws as it caterwauled. Mr. Jones leaped toward Mrs. Jones and managed to yank it off her back by sheer strength of will and put it back into the tub. He helped hold the creature in place while Mrs. Jones finished rinsing it.

After she drained the tub of its murky water, she lavishly covered the demon in conditioner and turned on the tap. It started and hissed, trying to climb her again. She and Mr. Jones grabbed for its scruff, realizing too late that conditioner made it nearly impossible to hold. It bolted for the top shelf of the towel cupboard. There it sat, hissing and shrieking, swatting at them every time they reached for it. "Now maybe a good time for a break, Mrs. Jones," Mr. Jones said. "I believe you both could use one."

Mr. Jones turned off the water in the bathtub and carefully reached for a washcloth in the cupboard. Turning on the tap in the sink, he gingerly began to clean the various wounds on Mrs. Jones's arms and shoulder. Her blouse was soaking wet and stained with blood. Streaks of red adorned the vanity and the near side of the bathtub like macabre Christmas garland, and drops seeped into the towel on the floor. It looked more like butchering day than bath time.

"Are you alright, Marjorie?" Mr. Jones asked.

Mrs. Jones felt her center shift. She could not recall the last time Mr. Jones had called her by her first name. She looked up into his lined face and saw a tenderness that was like an old friend come to visit.

"I am, Henry," she smiled. "Are you?"

"Oh, I'm just fine," Mr. Jones said, "but I do believe that demon is shivering."

The demon sat high on the shelf, visibly shaking with cold. "I summoned it. I am responsible for it," she sighed.

Without hesitating, she grabbed the slippery demon and plunked it into the bathtub. She started the water and checked the temperature while the demon shivered and hissed and scratched at her already damaged arms. When the warm water flowed from the cup over the trembling demon's slimy fur, it didn't run away this time. It growled low in its throat and glared with evil intention at her, but it sat still and let her rinse it.

Mr. Jones couldn't help but admire his wife's skillful handling of the creature and her singular determination. This lively woman was the one he remembered falling in love with.

When she finished, Mrs. Jones opened the folded towel and threw it over the demon. She wrapped it around the creature as she lifted it out of the bathtub and began rubbing it dry. Mr. Jones had never seen a creature with a more murderous look in its eyes than this very demon at this very moment, but it held still for a short time. Then Mrs. Jones unceremoniously dumped it out of the towel onto the floor. It landed on its feet, hissed, and began licking itself in various places about its body.

Mr. Jones wondered if he should let on to his wife that he knew the demon was, in fact, a cat. Once again, the weight filled his belly, and he wondered was she losing her grip on reality or was this an attempt to trick him. After all, he had said no dogs, he had said no cats, but he had never said no demons. Either way, perhaps it would be best if he allowed her this concession.

When Mrs. Jones opened the bathroom door, the waterlogged demon cat stalked out. Her arms were battered and bloody, and her shirt was soaked through, but Mrs. Jones's eyes shone with the light of someone full of tenderness. Mr. Jones's chest twinged with love.

"It seems we have a pet demon now, Mrs. Jones," Mr. Jones said, taking her hand.

Care Chain

Samia Selene Fakih

HAVE YOU EVER THOUGHT ABOUT CARE LIKE A CHAIN?

AND WHICH LINK IS YOU?

IF YOUR PARTNER IS CARING FOR THEIR MOM...

YOU CAN'T DO IT ALL ALONE. NONE OF US CAN.

AND YOU'RE CARING FOR YOUR PARTNER...

WHO'S CARING FOR YOU?

THAT'S WHY CARE IS LIKE A CHAIN. WE ALL LINK TO EACH OTHER.

WE GOT YOU!

AH, THANKS!

North Star

Erin Fries Taylor

He grabs the dusty cardboard box and bustles down the attic ladder and into the living room. I follow. Already unwrapping each wooden figure from the tissue-paper cocoon that is theirs for eleven months of the year, he announces each one's arrival. Though he bears the same name as the scene's father figure, my son is drawn not to that one but to those bearing gifts. "They're far away now, but will find Him eventually," he notes, offering more wisdom than he realizes. Finishing, he begins to hum just as the sun breaks through clouds and streams into the room.

The Improbability of Believing in Santa Claus

E.F. Sweetman

D *id you find out about Santa?"*
My eighth birthday fell in early December
1970. I was the middle child of five, and I was
definitely *that kid* in my family. The one who got others
in trouble, who slipped in and out of the house without
anyone noticing, the one who decided to take a look under
my parent's bed just before my birthday.

I could not believe what I found! I hit the birthday
jackpot. Bags and boxes of so many things. Stuffed
animals, a Barbie kitchen carousel, ski sweaters with
matching hats in different colors, paint and colored pencil
sets, books, board games, and a macrame owl kit.

I had no idea why my mother decided to make my
eighth birthday a banner year, but I was totally cool with

it. I probably felt like a banner year was long overdue. The reality that the number of presents was enough for five kids, and many were multiples of the same thing in five different sizes, never dawned on me. Nor did I take into consideration that Christmas was just a couple of weeks away because I one hundred percent believed that Santa Claus brought the presents. No, as I rooted through a staggering amount of gifts, I was certain everything was for me.

I was not only shocked to see an appropriate pile of gifts on the kitchen table on the morning of my birthday but the reality of what I discovered finally dawned upon me. The loot under the bed was for Christmas. Presents for all of us children. Which meant my parents were Santa Claus. Turning eight was a banner year, but not the reality I had hoped.

Fortunately, in my misery, I had company. I went to a neighborhood school. Our classes were small, everyone knew everyone. When we grouped together for gym, music, and art we shared everything we learned about life. In our combined classes, we dished out the latest. Second grade was the year many of my other classmates 'found out about Santa.'

As Christmas drew near, the big question was, "Did you find out about Santa?" There were only two answers:

1. The *Sad Yes* or
2. The *Wide-Eyed What?*

I was a *Sad Yes*, but I believe the question was

tougher on the *Wide-Eyed Whats?* because they got either "There is no Santa!" or worse, "You still believe in Santa? AHAHAHAHAHA!" Sometimes they got both, and yes, there were tears.

By the beginning of third grade, the Santa Question was out because we moved on to a very hot topic of the Mystery of Where Babies Came From. The Santa Question did not even come up in December because we assumed everyone knew the truth until the day our music teacher was late for the Christmas Pageant rehearsal.

The rule was to wait quietly until the teacher showed up, which never happened. We used the time to gossip our heads off. That day we discovered that one of our classmates, Kenny, who was absent, still believed in Santa.

Kenny was a regular kid. Good at math, he had a paper route, he usually got picked second or third for kickball. Then, for whatever reason that only makes sense to third graders, we decided we would keep Kenny believing. In case there was any doubt, Carl, the biggest kid in class (probably because he was at least two years older than the rest of us) laid down the law. He stood on his chair and declared: "Nobody! Tell Kenny! About Santa!"

We did not tell Kenny about Santa. On top of that, we all acted as if Santa was real again. In doing so, we got back some of the magic that felt lost.

We managed to "Keep Kenny Believing" through fourth grade as well. It was a great day when word circulated just after Thanksgiving that Kenny still believed. Again, we all acted as if Santa was real. It was fun to pretend. I thought as I watched him deliver our paper on a snowy afternoon that he was lucky yet so tragic to still believe. His day would come.

Which it did in fifth grade. We were at indoor gym, playing dodgeball. Hard-core dodgeball. With that red ball that made a loud boink! sound when it peened off your head and felt like a slap if you got it in the back. Our classmate Daryl was the reigning champion. Pure athleticism and grace on the court, he either caught the ball no matter how hard it was thrown or managed to make impossible leaps and pirouettes to just miss getting hit.

That fateful day should have gone down as "The Day Daryl Got Beat at Dodgeball" if the following never happened: Kenny threw an easy shot at Daryl, which - shocking to all of us- Daryl dropped! And with that, the Dodgeball King had fallen. The gym went quiet until Kenny started to whoop and run around. So we all followed, whooping, jumping, and running around Daryl sitting on the floor sulking with his head on his arms and knees.

Our gym teacher, Mr. Kyle stopped our nonsense by blasting his whistle three times, the signal to line up at the door. We were supposed to be quiet and orderly before we left the gym, but we were too giddy and we kept up the celebration until Daryl had enough. He turned to Kenny and shouted, "So what! Who cares? You're so stupid, you still believe in Santa Claus!"

We were in shock. Kenny looked confused.

"Shut up Daryl!" Carl shouted.

"Daryl's joking," said Michael.

Their words only solidified the truth of what Daryl had said. Kenny looked at all our faces, then shook his head. It was a crushing blow for Kenny. It was a crushing blow for all of us.

As we filed back to class, our teacher, Miss Richards said, "What's the matter with you all? You're never this quiet."

§§§

It did not strike me until years later how remarkable it was. We acted in a selfless, protective manner, without adult guidance. We protected one of our own to protect something we once had. If a parent or teacher told us to make sure Kenny kept believing in Santa, we would have beat one another up to be the first to blow it for him. None of that dawned on me until I had my own kids, but I want them to have something beyond lists of things and piles stuff. Not all is lost after things change when you make something special for another person.

At the Tapas Restaurant, Two Tables of Girlfriends Each Performing Scenes from Sex in the City

Colleen Michaels

When the plates start arriving
we allow the fiddleheads their modesty,
curled in tight like most green spring things.
They've turned their backs to us like freshman girls
who know the trick of taking off a bra
without showing anything.

We are seasoned enough to find them charming,
not put off by these new fresh belly buttons,
and we hold back on salting our tender skins.

When the table next to us orders cava
we encourage them in their bravado.
They are celebrating. The prettiest one,
and they are all pretty, has turned twenty-eight.
Opening wide they position their throats under the Peron
like hungry birds waiting for mothers to feed them.

We are tender enough to find them charming,
not put off by these new fresh belly buttons,
and we hold back on salting our seasoned skins.

Drugstore

Susanna Baird

She's sorry if she seems out of it, she just got back, she was gone. Gone to New York, her son passed away, it was his birthday and she and her daughter went, see here are the photos, this is his gravestone, it was his birthday, she went to New York. They went, here's her daughter, see, and her other two sons and the little one in the right-hand corner, that's her son who passed. It was his birthday and they went. She went and now she's back, scanning disinfectant wipes, bug spray, and a bottle of generic pain relief.

Bus 10

Jim DeFilippi

He drove a bus for the elderly and disabled for ten years as his retirement job, before the cancer hit. His dispatcher, Mikey, was divorced and did some of the scheduling. She used her paycheck to keep horses, up in the Islands. The driver asked her, "Mikey, can you get me some extra rides this week, next week? As many as you can of these, from this list here. There's some people I want to say goodbye to."

"You leaving?" Mikey was sitting at the console with headphones covering one ear. She nodded up at him and took the piece of paper he was handing across the counter to her.

"Many as you can please, if you can, Mikey. You can't get everybody. I wrote them down for you."

155

She nodded up at him again. The radio squawked and she waved him off.

He could still see the faces of every one of his favorite clients. They weren't called "riders" or "customers" or "patients"—they were clients. He had rolled them in wheelchairs, helped them unfold their walkers, searched for crutches and canes under the seat. Driven them to dialysis, adult daycare, doctors' appointments, hair salons and shopping. Sometimes they asked him to just drive around, although he had to give the office an official destination and a reason for the ride. They were all still there in his rearview mirror.

§§§

Ina Kahn was pushing ninety, rode to dialysis three times a week, except on Jewish holidays, when she walked the three miles, both ways. She had named her pickup truck Geronimo, but she couldn't drive it anymore because when they tried to take her license, she had hidden it away and couldn't remember where.

Ina's neighbors worried about her whenever she trimmed the ten-foot hedge in front of her house. They told her she was going to fall off that ladder and hurt herself. They wanted to do it for her. So at two in the morning, she put on a flashlight hat, plugged in the electric-clippers, and climbed up the ladder in the dark.

Her family wanted to take away her power of attorney. Their lawyer told her, "Ina, you can't write checks anymore, you're just mostly blind. You can't even see my face right now, can you?"

"I can see your mustache and the dollar signs in your eyes."

She was five foot even. The driver gave her a kiss on the top of her head as she shuffled in to be hooked up to the machine.

§§§

Steve Kahn was no relation to Ina, as far as the driver could tell. He would take Steve to stock shelves at Healthy Living, down on Dorset Street. Every morning Steve would say, "I drive," and he would pretend to slip his way into the driver's seat. That got the both of them laughing, every time.

Steve could say words but he had trouble building them into sentences. He'd say, "Birthday." You'd tell him. Then he'd ask, "Year," and when you told him, he'd said, "Thursday" or "Sunday" or whichever. And he was right every time, for anyone you could think of.

Steve had all the World Wrestling Federation videos, Volumes I through XVII.

The driver shook hands with Steve, grabbing and holding with both hands, and told him, "Don't work too hard today, buddy."

§§§

Bill Noeltz knew everything about *I Love Lucy*. When the driver had asked him about Lucy's neighbor, the lady, Bill told him it was Ethel Mertz, played by Vivian Vance. Bill told him where and when Vivian was born.

"Bill, do you watch those on DVD?"

"What? Dick Van Dyke?"

At Tower Community Services, the driver gave Bill a thumbs-up as he headed in.

§§§

Twelve-year-old Benjamin Ford-Harris couldn't talk and he couldn't move, but you could tell he was smart and funny and at peace with the way things were. The driver would sing Willy Nelson to him as they drove to Ben's middle school.

On the Road Again.

"Ben, you're the only one who never complains about my singing."

The little muscles around Ben's mouth and eyes would start grinning at that.

Ben's aide took over when the lift came down and she rolled him into the school.

The diver climbed back into the van and swiveled the handle to close the door. "All my life is making music with my friends, just can't wait to get on the road again."

§§§

Maida had been a Vermont farm wife her whole life. Simple, quiet, proud. A print house dress and a face out of Norman Rockwell. One time, when a cop car pulled up beside them at a light, she yelled up to the driver, "Look who's here. You can smell him."

Like some punk on a street corner.

So he hadn't been too surprised the time she asked the other three farm wives on their way to daycare, "Girls, have you ever wanted to punch someone in the mouth as hard as you could?"

He figured the question to be rhetorical, but all three started telling their stories about punching someone in the mouth. He was the only one without a story.

Skip Coffey would drive Maida back home each afternoon, in Bus 7. She called him "Drink Tea."

This last ride, the driver told Maida, "Tell Skip goodbye for me." She ignored him.

§§§

Herb drove Bus 35. He was even older than the driver.

You could never understand a word Herb said over the radio, but every one of his transmissions would end with a very clear and emphatic, "God damn it!" That was Herb's code for sign-off, his end punctuation mark.

"Base to Thirty-five, Herb, what's your twenty?"

"Kra-spilot-gratchet, *God damn it*!"

"Base did not copy that, Herb, your 10-9 for us

please, where are you?"

"I said glug-gutch-peequo, *God damn it!*"

§§§

Donald's father had been the Vermont Golden Gloves Welterweight Champ. When Donald was a kid, each November his father would take him, along with the over-under 12 gauge and a pocket of shotgun shells, to go hunting in the Vermont woods.

For Christmas trees.

They would spot a twenty-foot spruce and blast off the top six feet.

Donald used to be a Town Constable, but if he spotted any trouble, he'd just go home.

The driver nodded to Donald and put up his dukes, like a prizefighter. Donald did that too. They both were grinning.

§§§

One time, the driver had taken a client he didn't know out to the hospice house at Taft's Corners. Delivering him there to die. Where was his family? The guy told jokes the whole way.

§§§

Mr. Sayre never spoke a word, two rides a week, for years. The driver figured he must be mute. One day on

Joy Drive, Mr. Sayre called up to him from the back, "Bob Hope died."

The driver gently touched Mr. Sayre's back as he went in for his session.

§§§

The funniest client, an ex-realtor named Schmitt, eventually got Alzheimer's and couldn't leave the house anymore. Both his brothers had died.

§§§

That was the only bad thing about the job. Nobody lived long enough.

But the driver figured they were all still sitting back there, their faces reversed in the rearview mirror and smiling up at him. He would try to keep his eyes on the road as he called back over his shoulder, "Hey, let me know if I missed any bumps, okay? I'll go back and get them for you."

§§§

Now, Bus 10 pulls up to the steps. The new driver is twenty-two, working until he can make enough to take courses full-time. He casually grabs onto the slide handle and swings the door open without getting up, like you're supposed to. He calls out, "You okay there? You need any help?"

The old man snaps a military salute. "Request permission to come aboard, sir."

"What?"

The old man grabs both handrails and pulls himself up the three steps without looking at the new driver.

"North Shore Hospice for you?"

"That's right."

"You visiting somebody?"

The old man doesn't answer. He takes small steps to the first seat behind the driver, sits, and pulls himself over to the window, then clips himself in.

When the bus pulls out into traffic, he calls up to the front, "So, how's Bus Ten been treating you?"

Nate and Keegan Ollis
Jill Pabich

Heroic Care

In 2012, 10-year-old Keegan Ollis lost his father Nate, a soldier in the U.S. army who had two weeks left to go before being discharged. He was stabbed to death in a drug-related murder while still on active duty in Seattle, where he was seeking medical treatment. Nate's feet had been shattered by an IED when he was fighting the war in Afghanistan, and he came home unable to walk. He was awarded a Purple Heart.

A good friend of mine had fought in Iraq and I felt compelled to do something to give back to the people who had risked their lives in those senseless wars. I contacted Snowball Express, an organization that helps support families and children of fallen soldiers. They ask artist volunteers to donate their time and talent to create portraits of soldiers killed in action to give to their families. They connected me with Lisa Ollis, Nate's sister, who had adopted Keegan when his dad died. She brought me photos and other materials in order to paint Nate's portrait. It was to be a gift to Keegan. We all decided that Keegan should also be in the portrait, so I photographed him when they visited my studio.

In the painting, I tried to show the connection between Nate and Keegan by having it look like Nate was singing to Keegan. The flag in the picture has one gold star, which represents a fallen soldier who served with honor. (A blue star represents a soldier on active duty. Tragically, some flags have two gold stars). After the visit to my studio, Lisa asked me to include a cardinal. After they left, one followed their car for a distance, and Keegan was sure it was his dad's spirit. I hope it was.

I haven't been in touch with Lisa or Keegan in some years, and Keegan is now 17. He's almost old enough to enlist in the army, as was his and his aunt's plan for him. I hope no more portraits need to be painted.

The Visit

Ian P. Owens

I wait, masked as they wheel her out. Six feet away, also masked, a shrunken white thing. In clothes I've never seen before. I tell her my name. She repeats it, as a question. She had a stroke, they said. Maybe more than one. I tell her all my news, to fill up the twenty minutes allowed. I say other names: her sister still living, her husband long dead. No response. Then our eyes meet. No one else has my mom's eyes. So cold, so savage. They say: Who is this person? I'm thinking the same thing. That hasn't changed.

Aasia

Maria Daversa

J *e suis ici pour voir Chloé DiSalvo."* I'm nervous, and I speak too fast. I say I'm here for my daughter. The man hovers in the doorway. He can't be more than eighteen, nineteen tops. He's tall and wiry with dark skin and short hair. It's bright orange, a carrot orange. A bad dye job doesn't begin to describe how it looks.

"Je suis sa mère." I'm her mother, I say. *"Je veux la voir."* I tell him I want to see her, and I shove my foot in the door.

He kicks it out of the way.

I grab the door handle and battle with him to keep it open. I didn't come all this way to be shut out of my daughter's life now.

He eyes me. It's sharp. It's a warning. *"Je sais qui*

169

tu es." He says he knows who I am and releases the
door enough for me to slip inside. When he finishes
reconfiguring the locks, he sidesteps me and gives me a
good look before he shakes his head and strolls off.

I follow him down the hall. Cockroaches run
straight up the walls, unwashed dishes line the kitchen
counters, hash pipes, papers, and scales cover the dining
room table. A twin-sized mattress eclipses a doorway. It's
old and soiled, and most of it blocks the entry to the room
as if someone thought it could impersonate a door. Two
white toddlers play in the tiny space beneath it like it's
normal, or proper, or safe. This place is a multicultural
study about how not to raise children.

We enter the living room, and I check my watch
and comb the space for Chloe, but I don't see her. A four-
year-old flies past me and runs for the couch. She's wearing
pajama bottoms and an adult-sized t-shirt with *LES BLEUS*
on it. She drags a Barbie doll by its arm, a white-skinned
model with blond hair if it can still be called hair. Most
of it's been plucked out. The girl scales the couch, but her
legs get tangled in the shirt, and she tumbles to the floor.
Undeterred, she throws the doll, grabs on to the cushions,
and hoists herself up. She crawls between two men already
there, both of whom are slumped in some degree of prone.

A second child, possibly eighteen months, enters
the room behind her. She has on a diaper and nothing else.
Dark circles edge the skin beneath her eyes, and her long
ebony hair spills down her back in an unusual array of first-

class sailor's knots.

Every muscle of my being constricts. Chloe said her daughter is a year-and-a-half. Could this be—is this Aasia? I want to ask the man, but I don't have the words. Maybe I don't want to know.

The younger girl races for the couch, hops onto her tippy toes, and delivers an ear-splitting scream. Several young women in upholstered armchairs watch TV; they're half asleep. A man reclines on a second couch. No one pays any attention to her.

Tears sting my eyes. Where the hell is my daughter?

The four-year-old hoots and taunts the little one with Forlorn Barbie. The eighteen-month-old reaches across the cushion, snatches the doll, and chucks it. It lands on the rug inches in front of her. She belts out another high-pitched shriek.

Still, no one hears her.

My escort eases himself into a tattered old La-Z-Boy and lights up a cigarette. A stack of medical books sits on the floor beside the chair. They're old and the bindings are held together with bright blue duct tape. There's also an open notebook with a bunch of writing about microbiology. Carrot Head is a medical student?

"Où est Chloe?" I ask.

"Your daughter is not here." His voice is hoarse. It's no more than a whisper.

I want to explain how this can't be true, how Chloe called me last night and said she wants to come home when

171

the eighteen-month-old distracts me. She lies at my feet and plays with the doll. She swivels around on her stomach, then rolls on her back and sings to herself. She flies the toy above her head as if it's an airplane.

"I'm here to get her and her daughter," I say.

It's as if he doesn't hear me. He's focused on the sixty-inch, flat-screen television on the other side of the room. A European version of another exploitive home shopping channel blares out to no one in particular.

"She had some business this morning," he says.

"Business?" I finger my turtleneck. I can't get enough air.

The child on the floor finishes her song, sits up, and hammers the doll headfirst into the carpet. Not satisfied with this, she pounds it into the rug until both of its legs snap off. It's like she has a tiny motor inside of her that won't shut off. Giddy with laughter, she springs to her feet. She looks at me, but she doesn't see me. She doesn't see me. She's not even two, and she's detached and afloat in the world. She's a baby, and she wears the dulled expression of the walking dead like she's a war veteran, or a car accident victim, or an earthquake survivor.

"You speak to me like I am a terrorist," he says. "Or a jihadist like you see on the news."

Now I'm the one who pretends to be hard of hearing. I scan the room again. Maybe this guy has it all wrong. Maybe Chloe is here, and I didn't see her.

"Not everyone who lives in the banlieues is an

extremist."

I fall back on my social work training, hoping he'll have some sympathy for me. See how worried I am about my daughter and help me out. "I hear your anger," I say.

"Is that so, Snow White?"

"I suppose you're the one who . . . got my daughter pregnant." I can barely utter the statement.

He laughs and takes one more drag. "No." He lets the smoke escape his lips. "I am not."

"So, who is he—the father of her child?"

"You are as I thought you would be."

"I don't even know what that means." I fidget with my bracelet. The sapphires are as cold as dry ice.

"You do not understand."

"That's not fair," I whine like a child. I want to explain myself, say the right things that will make me forgivable in his eyes, that will make him disclose my daughter's whereabouts and when she'll return, but the eighteen-month-old charges past me again. She flings herself at the couch, squirms across the cushions, and pinches the older girl who slaps her hand away and kicks at her. The little one screeches again, and it sets ablaze all of my humiliation for being a shit lousy mother. I never thought it'd go this far.

The little one drops to the rug in front of the couch.

A white-hot inferno of rage blasts through me. "What about this child's parents?" I ask. "If I'm the one who doesn't understand, enlighten me about why no one is here to dress this child, or brush her hair, or wash the juice stains off her face?"

Carrot Head grins at me. "You are certain you want to know the story of this child's family?" he asks.

I narrow my eyes.

He positions the cigarette between his teeth and inhales again. The smoke unfurls from his lips with the unhurried nature of a man in control. "This girl's mother," he meets my glare, "is your daughter, and she is out trying to score."

"Oh, God." It's true. My daughter has relapsed.

This is her baby.

This is Aasia.

My heart plummets. I slip a fingernail under the cuff of my sleeve and gouge at the unhealed lesions on my wrist, but this grief goes too deep, and no amount of scratching will relieve it.

"I recognize Chloe better now," he says. "The reason she is a junky."

"Don't say that, damn you. Don't you say that about her."

"How many years can you treat someone as if they do not exist?"

"I had problems, terrible problems when I raised her."

"So I have been told."

"I don't know what my daughter said to you—"

"Your daughter suffers. She needs someone to love

her."

Love. It's all my daughter ever wanted, yet it's the one thing I wasn't able to give her.

"What's your name?" I ask.

He draws lightly on the cigarette; his attention returns to the TV. "Jibreel," he says.

"Well, Jibreel." I force a smile. It's sheepish. "When does my daughter come back from . . . you know . . . when she goes out like this?"

"Who can say?" The muscles in his jaw stiffen. He grinds his teeth. "When she runs out of money, she will come home."

"This is not her home!" My eyes burn—tears stream down my face.

Jibreel says no more. He's done with me. He stubs out his cigarette and slumps farther into the chair. The four-year-old scampers over to him, and he repositions himself so she can climb in his lap. She rests her head on his chest and points at the pretty lady hawking the overpriced stainless-steel food dehydrators.

A flurry of single syllables flashes through my frontal lobe. Hide. Fight. Cry. Run.

What about the girl?

She's not my problem.

I can't leave her here.

I can't care for her either. I didn't do such a hot job with my daughters.

At the very least, I can find something for her to

wear.

I approach Aasia.

She's sprawled across the couch. Her inner motor is idle at the moment.

I take off my sweater and drape it across her shoulders, and our eyes meet—we connect, and she *sees* me. She hops off the couch and pokes her twig-like arms through the sleeves. She tries to run from me, but I snag her by her armpits and balance her on my hip. "How about we find you a cute outfit to go with your new sweater?" I ask.

She sucks her finger and studies my face. I lower her to the carpet and let her find her footing. I hold out my hand, and she takes it and pulls me in the direction of her room. Her heels pound the carpet as she stomps down the hall and drags me into what she believes is an actual bedroom. The space is empty, save for an unmade bed. The closet is empty too. So is the bureau. The whole freaking room is a cavity except for a pile of sheets heaped in the middle of the floor.

I want to scream.

I crawl around on all fours and search for anything that resembles clothing when I discover an old, crumpled t-shirt under the bed. It's black with "Car Doctor" written in big white letters across the front. I haul it out, and the girl raises her arms so I can dress her in it. It looks ridiculous, but it'll have to do. She searches my face and smiles at me. I run my fingers through her ratty hair and imagine braiding it into a crown on top of her head.

Maybe I can take her with me. I'll buy her some decent clothes and cook her a burger. I'll return for Chloe tomorrow when my daughter is sober and reasonable, and we can work out a plan to raise this child together.

I failed Chloe once. I can't fail my granddaughter.

"I know where we can find a whole new outfit for you to wear," I say. "Do you want to come with me?"

She nods her head so hard I'm afraid she'll hurt herself. I reach for her, and she climbs into my arms and squeezes her legs around my waist. Her bony heels stab me in the back, but I don't say anything, and I don't stop her because I can't remember the last time I held a child this secure or this close to my heart. I have her like this as we creep down the hall. When we reach the front door, I fumble with the locks and pray no one hears us.

A bottle falls in the kitchen and rolls across the linoleum.

It startles me, and I freeze. I wait. Aasia meets my gaze.

Someone swears at it and picks it up.

The girl fondles a strand of my hair. She holds it against her cheek, then flings it in the air.

I glance around the hallway, but there's no place for us to hide. Jibreel is at the counter. He has his back to me.

Aasia swings her foot, and I'm pretty sure it connects with my kidney. I make an ouchy face, and she gives me a big got-cha grin. I rest my finger on her lips.

Jibreel opens the refrigerator and removes another

bottle. He twists off the cap, flicks it, and it skids across the floor.

What if he sees me, with Aasia—

He steps out of the kitchen, and we lock eyes. I hold my breath, and time stands still, and a lifetime of excuses about all the ways I should've treated my daughter better tear through my brain. I can only pray that I'm not too late.

His eyes settle on the girl.

I hold Aasia tight.

Seconds pass. He drops his gaze and moves off toward the living room.

I exhale, but we continue to wait. We wait and see if anyone gets suspicious because they don't see Aasia's knotted head roaring up and down the hall. I wait and see if someone worries because the wild girl's doll is in pieces across the living room rug, but she is nowhere to be found. I wait and see if at least one of these individuals gets concerned because the one sound in the room is the television, and the child who can stop a crowd hasn't let one loose for a while. No one does any of these things, but it's okay.

We're going home.

I give Aasia a peck on the cheek, and she wraps her skinny arms around my neck. I hug her with everything in me, finish with the locks, and we slip out of the apartment. I close the door behind us.

Grandson

After Jamaica Kincaid's "Girl"

Susanna Baird

Sticks stay outside; you are not a dog. Boots stay in the
mudroom; this is not the Wild West. Always ask for a
guest's coat; never ask for a guest's shoes. Manners before
mud. Be the first to offer your hand. Be the last to take a
second helping. Open the door for your grandmother; I
expect it. Don't open the door for your aunt; She resents
it. Don't ask me why. Don't hit your sister. *But she said
I …* Don't interrupt. If it's urgent, say "excuse me." If
your sister hits you, you deserve it. No means no; I don't
care what you thought she was saying. Clam chowder is
milk and potatoes, not broth and tomatoes. Boil lobster in
seawater and serve with drawn butter. Never eat shellfish
in a month without an R. Always eat shellfish with vodka,
preferably in a Bloody Mary. Horseradish not Old Bay.
Celery not jalapeno. Always have the first drink. Never
have the third. Nobody likes a sloppy drunk or corn from
New Jersey. *I'm not old enough …* Don't interrupt. If
it's urgent, say "excuse me." Philanthropy not charity.
Baseball not football. Station wagon not SUV. J. Press
not Brooks Brothers. English setter not golden retriever.
Vinalhaven not the Vineyard. Don't pick your nose; that's
what Swamp Yankees do. Pick a woman for her bottom
and her brain, not her chest and her laugh. Good ankles
are not to be overlooked. *Excuse me …* Don't interrupt;
it's not urgent unless your pants are on fire. Marry for love

and a shared literary sensibility. Stay married for friendship and tennis. The Wall Street Journal is not literary. Golf is not tennis. Sex is important and don't let anyone tell you money is not. When you talk, speak up. Don't mumble. Don't mince words. Don't talk with your mouth full. Don't talk politics or religion; it's crass, as is imitation maple syrup. Don't swear in front of your aunt; she thinks it's uncouth. Don't swear in front of your mother; she finds it low. If you're going to swear, commit to a proper epithet. Do not bother with the Lord, he's not worth your Sundays or the breath from your mouth. *Excuse me, could I try saying* … Your pants are not on fire and the answer is no. I don't care what you thought I was saying.

Dad

Deede Strom

I felt nervous as the storm intensified. Would we make it home? I felt Dad's hand on my shoulder. "Don't let a little rain scare you." He grabbed his big golf umbrella and walked us out on the tarmac. "Don't worry," he said. "I'll see you soon." Up the stairs I went, holding my toddler. For some unknown reason I stopped, holding up the line. There he was in the window, waving. Got home after a long flight. The next day my daddy died unexpectedly. I went out and stood in the rain, where no one could see my tears.

My Mother's Gift

Bobbi Lerman

W e are going to a special place today," my mother said.

My mother sat at the kitchen table beside me as I maneuvered spoonfuls of soup into my mouth. It was tomato, covered with a thin topping of crumbled Ritz crackers. It was just my mom and me eating soup. I don't recall where my older brother and younger sister were. I was four years old.

From where I sat, I could see the sharp pointed ends of the icicles hanging along the roof's edge. Snow covered the ground. Inside, a large wooden rack covered the heat register. Clothes of all colors were draped over it. My mom placed the empty bowls into the sink, then knelt beside me to put on my boots, coat, hat, and mittens before wrapping

185

a scarf around my face so that only my eyes peeked out.
She laughed as she took my hand to step out onto the
sidewalk. I felt the heat of her skin against mine through
the thick wool of my mittens.

A short walk later we arrived in front of an
enormous brick building in the center of the square a
few blocks from our home. Outside the door, my mother
crouched in front of me and whispered words I'll never
forget:

"This is where the magic lives, Bobbi."

Heavy oak doors opened to reveal two large rooms.
Ceiling to floor shelves were filled with books. I had never
seen so many. I remember wondering to whom they all
belonged and if I was going to be allowed to look at any of
them. As we took off our coats and hung them on a metal
rack, my mother explained how one whole section of this
library was set-aside for children.

I liked the idea of a place just for someone like me.

Small tables and chairs were scattered in the farthest
corner of the smaller room. Large windows lined an entire
wall. Sunlight bounced off every surface. I couldn't take
my eyes off the large desk in the middle of the room or
the lady with gray hair who sat behind it. A pile of books
towered above her on each side.

It was so quiet. Not like home with, not just my
mother and father, brother and sister, but, also aunts,
uncles, and cousins, too many to count who lived on the
other two floors. A house always filled with voices, talking,

most often shouting to be heard over one another, doors slamming and feet stomping up and down the floors of the three family we all lived in. The reasons everyone spoke in whispers here must be because they did not want to scare the magic away.

My mother led me to a table under a window of colored glass. Within a few moments, the gray-haired woman brought over a pile of books of all different shapes. My mother picked up the top book and opened it, telling me in a soft voice that the name of it was *Sleeping Beauty*. I hung on every note in her voice as she wove the tale of the princess who slept a hundred years until her prince awakened her with a kiss.

Each day after, no matter the weather, we walked to the library after my lunch. Always the two of us, always with her warm hand in mine as we made our way to the brick building filled with books and quiet. It was there in that room under the stained-glass window where my mother taught me to read. It was there she gifted me with an ability to find the wonder and magic in the world around me.

I journeyed to many different places from our little table. I met many people. Among them were Anne of Green Gables, and Mary, a little girl who journeyed on her own from India to her uncle's home in northern England to discover a secret garden that brought life back to everyone who lived there. I met one hundred and one dalmatians and tigers and lions and bears. I soared high with Ali Baba on his enchanted carpet. The words on the page took me back in time and forward. My mother and I traveled the globe and beyond. Every afternoon I was swept away from the corner where we sat to the entrancing, magical worlds of long ago and far away.

Between the reading of stories, we talked, we laughed, we shared dreams, we entrusted each other with secrets.

"All words hold a bit of magic," my mother explained. "How they are strung together or spoke determines the strength of the magic. Words help you find your way when lost. They can bring you home," she added. I didn't understand what she meant.

As I grew older, books became the only common ground between us. I received at least one new book from my mother on my birthday. The day I turned eleven, I came home from school to find a series called *The Adventures of Cherry Ames* waiting on my bed to be opened. For years after, I wanted to become a nurse – until I discovered I couldn't stand the sight of blood.

When I turned twelve, I received *Nancy Drew* mysteries. For a summer, I scoured the neighborhood pretending to be an amateur detective.

As I approached thirteen, I began to push at the protective boundaries my parents set down. Trips to the library with my mother became rare. Arguments between us were an almost daily occurrence. A few days before my birthday, I stomped out of the house in tears at my mother's refusal to allow me a day in Boston with two of my friends.

When I finally came home, she didn't say a word as I rushed past her and slammed the door to my room. I found a package on my bed. The note taped to it said, it was an early birthday present. It was a book with the title imprinted on the cover; *Anne Frank, The Diary of a Young Girl.*

The words in that book gave me my first glimpse of a world that existed beyond my own sheltered one; a world where happy endings weren't a guarantee and where mothers and fathers weren't always able to keep their children safe. Ann's story frightened me. Her story sent my emotions to a place of worry and anxiety they had never experienced. I needed my mother's calm, her reassurance that I was safe. It was her story that drew me back to the kitchen table where for a little while the magic of Ann's words closed the distance between my mother and myself.

The next day was my actual birthday. I returned home from school to find a small box wrapped with lavender paper placed on my bed. It was a diary. I opened it to find a message written on the inside cover in my mother's hand. "For your words, Bobbi and the magic I know you can create.

I started my first journal that day. Reading fostered the writer in me. Reading made me an inquisitive person. Reading fed my desire to learn about people, cultures, and places. Reading inspired me to reach high and to seek new experiences I might not have had otherwise.

I worked on a kibbutz in Israel. I backpacked across Europe. After each journey, I brought my mother a book about one of the places I had been. When I returned home from Israel, I brought her the story of one woman's experience during the Holocaust and her rebirth in modern-day Israel. After everyone had gone to bed, she made us tea and we sat at the kitchen table and talked.

I told her of my travels, of the people I'd met and the places I'd seen. I described the brilliant, almost unearthly color of the sunrise from the top of Masada and what I felt when I stood at what remained of the Western Wall of Solomon's Temple in Jerusalem as I place three notes there; one from my grandmother, one from my mom and my own, into the crevices of the ancient stones.

She chuckled when I described the sensation of floating in the salty Dead Sea. "I've no idea where you get this wanderlust of yours," she remarked.

I laughed at her puzzled expression. "Why from you, Mom," I replied. "Don't you remember?"

She looked at me for a long moment, and then, after a while, a knowing smile spread across her face. "I showed you were to find the magic."

During the long days my mother spent in the hospital for her chemo treatments, I read to her, hoping the magic, she loved would overcome the pain. For the first time, I read her some of my own words.

The last night I spent with her, she could not speak. Her eyes remained closed despite my urging. The morphine drip that eased her pain also rendered her into unconsciousness. I talked anyway. I read from some of her favorite books. I waited. I held her hand.

Her breathing changed around two in the morning. She grew restless and started to mumble. She called for her mother. She called out to go home. I whispered to her that it was okay, that we would all be fine. She should go if she wanted to.

Her finger's squeezed mine. "Remember the magic, Bobbi," she murmured.

My sister and brother arrived a few moments after. They offered to sit with her. Bone-tired, I went home. My mother died two hours later.

Throughout the year and a half of her illness before she succumbed to liver cancer, I couldn't allow myself to consider the possibility, let alone accept the reality that she would soon be gone from my life. There were days when the sound of her laugh sounded out so clear to me, I could swear my mother was standing in the room. After she died, the hurt remained too sharp and I pushed thoughts of her away, at least until this morning.

My family is still asleep as I watch the sun make its way above the horizon. A veneer of frost has collected on the window panes of my home overlooking Nahant Bay. Wind whistles, rattling the glass as it blows past unimpeded. The ocean is a deep, winter cobalt blue.

I sip on a steamy cup of Earl Grey and scrape mindless design on the icy coating of the window. The words thank you appear on the crystallized surface. For a long moment, all I can do is stare at the letter before the significance of my strange declaration becomes clear.

I am a writer. I am a writer in large part due to my mother's love of language and her enthrallment with the art of storytelling. My mother's special gift to me was the magic of words. I've never offered her the credit she was due. I can only hope she knows.

The anniversary of her death is a couple of weeks away. For once, the familiar rush of grief and pain does not accompany my remembrances. Memories are strange and at times it's like trying to find my way through a thick, swirling fog. Yet, each time I open a book and read the first words; I realize my mother is sitting there with me. She always will be. I can hear the lilting song of her voice in each story I read.

Orphans

Gail Gilmore

Your mama is dead, little ones.

I know the night she left you, the acrid scent of her death pulling me from the depths of dreaming. She is four nights gone,

never to return to the den beneath the linden tree—halfway between the wetland reeds and the place where humans live—

the den she dug to birth you, to shelter you from harm.

You are alone; vulnerable kits dressed in black and white, tumbling each over the other down the embankment, tottering through spring's moist earth, snuffling with baby breath through dried leaves. Then, later,

waddling, resolute, back up the embankment, five white-tipped tails slicing through green ground cover, then disappearing into the empty den to wait for what will never be.

Orphans

The sight of you shreds my heart.

And though I know what I know, still I hope. Hope it
wasn't her that night, wasn't a mama with kits.
At dusk, I walk down the embankment path to the linden
tree, sprinkle a handful of flour outside the den. Then,
like you, I wait in a state of hope for morning. But in the
morning there are no paw prints in the flour,

no reason for hope. She will not be back.

And since I cannot leave you to die, I remove you one by
one from the den, place you in a new one. Not as perfect
as the den your mama dug, but this one, too, is made with
love:

with the crate that transported my rescue dog home from a
Caribbean island; with shredded newspapers and soft, worn
towels to burrow in; with the double cocoon of a warm
wooden shed.

You are safe now. From coyotes and foxes, from owls and
hawks. From humans, who never seem to drive carefully
enough.

And I rest easier.

My cat shares his cans of wet food with you, as the wildlife
rehabber tells me it's the best thing to feed you.

And for the two weeks it takes me to find a rehab facility

for you, I watch you grow and thrive.

But when the day comes to load you and your crate-den
into my car, then drive 20 miles south to entrust your care
to the experts, I don't want to let you go.
Beguiled by the white crests of your small triangular heads,
the white blaze down the middle of your faces,

I've fallen in love.

But you are wild, your place in the world not with me. And
though some would try to tame your wildness to keep you
with them, I will not.

So we make that 20-mile drive, and

I watch the teen volunteers at the rehab center reach into
the crate with the faded "Live Animals: Handle With Care"
sticker, watch them scoop you up with delight,

watch even after the last volunteer has disappeared inside
and you are gone.

Lost

Lauren Zazzara

Streaks of blood smeared haphazardly on the coffee table, the hardwood, the duvet. My insides burst like fireworks. I watch myself as I run through the apartment, screaming her name. This is a movie and I am not me but someone paid to be me who doesn't quite know how to move in my body. Tearing through her hiding spots, calling my boyfriend, "Blood everywhere ... I can't find her ..." She suddenly emerges from the bedroom, the tip of her tail that she's been compulsively biting coated in crusted blood. I pull her into my arms and come back to life.

Walker

Betsy Ellor

M arcie's great with money…with spending it," Chase joked to the mayor, as he curled a proprietary paw around his wife's slim waist. Strings of incandescent light twinkled over the beach as the night breeze flapped the banner reading 'Grand Re-Opening.' On the temporary dance floor, silk gowns and white table cloths jostled for space with furs of brown, brindle, gold, and white. It was the dog's gala, too.

"I've never had a head for business," Marcie smoothed her blond french twist and didn't mention ten thousand dollars of the mayor's money she'd recently shifted into her private offshore accounts.

"That's the real reason women earn less than men. They don't fight for it. Take Marcie, Ivy League education and she's *a dog walker.*" Chase's mouth twisted sour.

"An excellent dog-walker," the mayor saluted her with his glass. Marcie looked coyly away and scratched the ears of the mayor's mastiff who had abandoned the mayor to sit beside Marcie.

It had been Chase who brought home two muscular, toothy Rhodesian Ridgeback puppies on a whim. Chase who had abandoned their training to Marcie the first time they trashed his Xbox room. She hadn't wanted them, but they needed her. Somehow, they became all she truly cared about. Full-grown now, Archer and Osprey lay curled around her feet; a copper brown hem to her emerald gown.

"Still! All her time spent on dogs! Why don't women realize money is power?"

Chase was man-ologuing now. She was used to it; a small price to pay. Chase made such an excellent cover. When she knew he wouldn't notice, Marcie twisted out of his grasp hoping he hadn't rumpled the perfect silk pleating at her waist. Her dogs following, she wandered the crowd, sipped champagne, and contemplated other things that have power like unsupervised access to people's homes, like evidence found of power abused that would ruin re-election, like photos taken and but not shared - for a fee.

Archer growled as a small, angry-looking man backed onto the hem of Marcie's dress.

"You're looking well," Marcie said.

"Yes, um, thanks," The Animal Control officer tugged his sleeves down, using them to dab sweat from his

pockmarked face. He was her first client - although he had
no pets. "Leashed, I see."

With a porcelain delicate hand, she held up the
two intricate leatherwork leashes that would do nothing to
stop her dogs, each ninety pounds of muscle tip to talon.
"Always," said Marcie, "It's the law."

It was at this very beach Animal Control taught
Marcie that law, back when swimming was the only way
to exhaust her insatiable puppies. All the dozen beaches
in town were for people only, not dogs, not ever. Animal
Control made that clear with a mountain of fines.

Marcie was forced to walk her pups twice as much
with them on leash. If her route took her past the beach
twin brown muzzles twitched with longing and sad eyelids
drooped over glittering eyes that broke her heart. Instead,
she routed her night walks past Animal Control's house,
and then through his yard, past his windows, taking pictures
of spoons and candles and needles. After that no more
fines.

It wasn't enough. Marcie had a taste for the
possibilities. After all, why should her dogs alone enjoy this
freedom? The next day she became a dog walker.

Animal Control stared with sunken eyes that flicked
for an escape. With a debutante's nod, she led her pack
away.

Drifting through currents of couture humanity
and designer dogs many of those she walked for nodded
politely. Others did not. The Zoning Board president with

a medicine cabinet full of opioid bottles labeled with other people's names, fled dragging an Airdale terrier that pulled to be with Marcie. The bank owner with a personal email full of white supremacist newsletters nodded with a stone smile that showed as much fang as friendship. They didn't like her, but their dogs loved her and she loved their dogs. Either way, they couldn't leave her for another walker, not if they wanted their secrets kept safe.

The glowing recommendations they gave their friends were a surprise, but misery always did love company. Perhaps they liked knowing the dirt she had on them would have company, stored with the dirt she had on everyone else.

Archer and Osprey jostled around her feet as she opened the ladies' room door into a cloud of expensive perfume. From the vestibule, Marcie heard the saccharine voice of the Influencer, "I know I haven't posted about it, but I've been taking my kids to this beach since they were born. Now it's for dogs! Off-leash! All the time! I don't know what this town is – Marcie!"

Bathed in the warm light, the Influencer held court on a tufted stool by the mirrors, yards of red lace pooled around her. The dress contrasted perfectly with the silky white of the Havanese, Bijou, pressed against the tight jeweled bodice.

Bijou jumped down and ran to her walker. After a quick scratch from Marcie, the three dogs began the usual bowing and sniffing to reconfirm their place in the pack order. Marcie glared a reminder at the Influencer; their agreement applied to what she said both online and out loud. "Bijou looks happy."

"He is, of course. A beach of his own! We're so excited," The Influencer forced a laugh, "It's marvelous really, just takes some getting used to. I hear Wingdrift beach will be the new hot spot … for, you know, humans."

Marcie said nothing. The other women waited, silent, watching. Finally, the Influencer floated up off her stool. "I really should be going."

Marcie took the forfeit throne. The Influencer and her troupe filed out. Marcie signaled Bijou to follow. Marcie got out her lipstick. She would never be as stunning as The Influencer. Then again beauty and pride led to sex-capades and videos locked in Marcie's safe.

When her make-up was flawless, Marcie paced the perimeter of the party. She ran a hand triumphantly over the sign she herself had designed and hung. "Dane Street Dog Beach." Voted in by a city council that could not risk refusing Marcie's petition. She smiled and escaped to the moonlit beach.

Marcie lowered herself onto the boardwalk, sand sifting through her chiffon skirt and sticking to her bare legs. Asher and Osprey flanked her, the pulse of them warm at her sides until she unclipped their leashes and they ran wild down the beach into the sea.

Marcie never intended to become her unique brand of entrepreneur. It was just that her puppies needed a beach, so she got them one. This beach, their beach. Archer and Osprey's muscles rippled as they ran down the sand, chasing their four-legged friends. Marcie started a mental list of other things she'd get for them, for all of them. It's amazing how easy it is to get things done when you've got a town by the leash.

"We're all just walking each other home."

- Ram Dass

Acknowledgements

Heroic Care is a testament to so many people who have cared about the project. For their help, I am eternally grateful.

I want to start by thanking Lauren Cepero for going above and beyond to help with the book cover design and the marketing material. All the marketing on this book is infinitely better thanks to her help. Also, Ralph Walker who gave me great advice about book promotion.

I want to thank Susanna, Liz, Bobbi, and Maria for fielding my endless text messages asking for ideas and second opinions. Jim DeFilippi was a fantastic publishing coach and answered my many questions with his vast wisdom.

Susanna Baird's excellent website Five Minutes (fiveminutelit.com) inspires me weekly. I'm grateful to Susanna for allowing me to include several pieces from the site here and encourage readers to go to the site to read more.

Of course, I also want to show appreciation to my husband, Nicholas, and my son, George, for their patience while I worked many more hours than I ever imagined on this project.

To all the contributors, both selected and not-selected I want to say thank-you. Writing truly is a labor of love and you all are heroic for fearlessly pursuing this work that you care about so deeply. I feel honored to have the opportunity to share your work with readers.

Susanna Baird

susannabaird.com

Susanna Baird is a writer living in Salem, Massachusetts.

Christi Byerly

awakencoaching.com

Christi Byerly, who's lived in six countries on three continents, runs Awaken Coaching. Her clients come from all over the globe.

Lara Bujold Clouden

elbycloud.wordpress.com

Lara's in Connecticut with her husband, two children and two dogs. She's lived in Duluth, New York, Paris, and outside San Francisco as a writer, editor, dancer, and business analyst.

Beth Anne Cooke-Cornell

Twitter: @BACookeCornell

Beth Anne Cooke-Cornell is a professor of writing and humanities at Wentworth Institute of Technology. She lives with her husband and three children in Salem, MA.

Maria Daversa

mariadaversa.com

Maria Daversa lives in the US and writes upmarket women's fiction. "Aasia" is her first fictional short story and adapted from her debut novel, Heirloom.

Jim DeFilippi

amazon.com/author/jimdefilippi

Jim DeFilippi has published more than thirty books, including crime fiction, humor, general fiction, history, stage drama, screenplays, even some poetry and a cookbook.

Kelley H. Dinkelmeyer

facebook.com/Kellfire-and-Brimstone

Kelly is a working mother - teaching university physics and raising a teenager with her husband. In between parenting, feeding the dog and cats, grading homework, and (sort of) cleaning the house, she sometimes jots down her thoughts or stories.

Tammy Donroe Inman

tammydonroe.com

Tammy Donroe Inman cooks and writes books in Waltham, MA.

Betsy Ellor

eellor.wordpress.com

Betsy has been both a dog walker and worked in a bar. Now she spends her days as Sr Editor for Words Unbound. When not writing she hikes and battles prehistoric mosquitoes in the woods of Massachusetts.

Samia Selene Fakih

samiaselene.com

Samia Selene Fakih (BFA Studio Art 2016, MFA Comics 2019) is an NYC-born illustrator. She edits comics by day and illustrates, writes, and draws her own comics at night.

Gail Gilmore

gailgilmoreauthor.com

Gail Gilmore is the author of the memoir Dog Church, and a volunteer for Missing Dogs Massachusetts. She lives in New Hampshire with her spouse and rescue dog.

Sandra Hudson

Sandra is a semi-retired nurse, former business owner and entrepreneur. Her role as a mother, wife and grandmother brings her joy and satisfaction. She loves to write and have done so most of my life. Painting, pottery, travel, and theatre are additional passions!

Susan Klobuchar

susanklobuchar.com

Susan Klobuchar is a redhead, mama, dog lover and ice cream enthusiast who tells stories that connect people. A believer in happy endings, she writes from Virginia's Blue Ridge Mountains.

Amos J. Landon

Amos lives in New Hampshire with his partner, five sons, two ferocious hedgehogs, and a turtle named Pickles. He writes fiction for children and adults with a focus on humor.

Bobbi Lerman

scribblersink.com

Bobbi Lerman's writing encompasses travel, personal essay, historical medieval romance. Bobbi is the founder of Scribbler's Ink, an active online facebook community.

Celine Mai

colorsofmai.com

Celine Mai is a mixed Vietnamese French illustrator living in New York with her family. Her comic "The Joy of Shopping" was published in *This Quarantine Life Anthology* in 2020.

Colleen Michaels

montserrat.edu/tag/improbable-places-poetry-tour/

Colleen Michaels hosts The Improbable Places Poetry Tour. In addition to being published in journals and anthologies, her poems have been made into installations for the Massachusetts Poetry Festival, the Peabody Essex Museum, and the Trustees of Reservations.

Elizabeth Montaño

facebook.com/Montano.Musings

A former journalist, Elizabeth Montaño now devotes her time to writing fiction and poetry and spending time with her family. To date, she has published eight novels.

Beth Price Morgan

facebook.com/elisabethpricemorgan

Beth Price Morgan is a writer and illustrator (by night) in Beverly, MA. By day, she directs Montserrat College of Art's Career Design Studio and chases her surprisingly fast 1-year-old.

Ian P. Owens

ianowens.com

Ian Owens is a self-employed engineer who writes for the fun of it, mostly about self-propelled travel and Vikings. His first book, called "Riding the Big One," has both.

Jill Pabich

Instagram: @jillpabichphotography

Jill lives in Salem with her family and way too many pets. She went to Tufts University and the Boston Museum School and is an award-winning artist and an amateur photographer. She is working on a spooky Middle Grade novel.

E.M. Panos

EM Panos is addicted to books & travel. She lives on Boston's north shore with her wife.

Matthew Phillion

matthewphillion.com

Matthew Phillion is the Salem-based author of the Indestructibles superhero series, the fantasy series the Dungeon Crawlers, and Echo and the Sea. He serves on the Salem Athenaeum's Writer's Committee.

Luna Ranjit

lunaranjit.medium.com

Luna Ranjit is a Nepali-USian writer who lives between Kathmandu and New York and moves between poetry and essays. Her work has appeared in Newtown Literary, The Margins, Truthout and elsewhere. She reads, writes, and dreams in four and a half languages.

Deede Strom

Deborah grew up north of Boston and enjoyed the ocean and the city. Today she calls the mountains of Vermont home. Deborah writes about the resiliency of the human spirit and things that touch our hearts.

E.F. Sweetman   bleakdarkcynical.home.blog

E.F. Sweetman writes crime, noir, horror and anthology from the North Shore of Massachusetts.

Ellen Symons   ellensymons.com

Ellen Symons lives in Lanark County, Ontario, Canada, surrounded by trees, fields, and animals. Ellen's published work includes the poetry collection, Economies of Gratitude. Ellen is working on a first novel.

Erin Fries Taylor

Erin lives in Annandale, Virginia with her husband, teen and tween boys, and two felines who preside over the household.

Young Vo   youngvoart.com

In the morning Young Vo writes and draws for kids. During the day he animates for the big kids. At night he acts like a kid.

Jill Witty   jillwitty.com

Jill Witty, an award-winning writer from Virginia and California, is currently writing a novel set in Italy. She holds degrees from Yale and UCLA

Marla Yablon
Twitter @MarlaYablon

Marla Yablon is a desert dweller who paints her world with words. She spends her days writing in the company of a large sulcata tortoise and an often bad-tempered cat.

Lauren Zazzara
lmzazzara.com

Lauren Zazzara is a writer in Buffalo, NY. When she isn't reading, (loudly) tapping at her keyboard, or napping, she is likely adoring her cat, Margaret.

Karen Zey
karenzey.com

Karen Zey's work has appeared in (mac)ro(mic), The Nasiona and other fine places. Karen lives in la belle ville de Pointe-Claire, Québec and leads writing workshops at her community library.

Mandy Zhang
Instagram: @mandywxz

Mandy Zhang is an illustrator based in Toronto Canada. Her drawings are simply drawn, sometimes with the use of everyday objects or pantry foods to create thought provoking images with minimalistic elements.

Words
Unbound

FIVE MINUTES
ONE HUNDRED WORDS

fiveminutelit.com

The following were all previously published on FiveMinuteLit.com